KU-741-732

Ebony and the Mookatook Bush

by Millie Murray

Illustrated by Judith Lawton

LONGMAN

CHAPTER 1

Ebony Louise Anderson loved calypso music. Any time of the day or night whenever the fancy took her she would be plugged up to her Walkman or her cassette player with her favourite music on. Her mother didn't mind that Ebony was absorbed in the music except when it interfered with her school work. If during the night Ebony had her cassettes playing her mother would be cross that she wasn't sleeping.

"Ebony, if you don't turn that music box off I'm taking it away from you." That was enough of a scare tactic to cause Ebony to press the STOP button.

Ebony was a great dancer too. Having a long mirror attached to her wardrobe was just right for her purposes. She would swing the door wide open and with the music turned up to a reasonable level (it depended whether her mother was in the house or not) she would prance round the room. All the while her eyes would be fixed on the mirror monitoring her movements. Ebony prided herself on being in time with the music – she was never out of beat. No matter if she had her eyes closed or she was singing so loud that she couldn't hear the music, she kept up with the rhythm. She even made up some of her own songs which she didn't share with anyone except the dolls and teddy bears which sat on her bed and on the top of her wardrobe. Her best song was "Fun in the Sun" which she had written at the beginning of the summer holidays. This is how it went:

"Everyone's having fun, fun, fun
Dancing under the sun, sun, sun
Moving to the beat, beat, beat
As they feel the heat, heat, heat."

Her teddy bear thought it was "wicked" (meaning excellent) and a few times when he watched Ebony dancing, he fell off the top of the wardrobe in excitement – with no bones broken, thank goodness!

One of Ebony's ambitions in life was to go to Trinidad – home of all carnivals and calypso music. Her parents came from the island of Jamaica which is known for its reggae music. Ebony liked this music too, but it couldn't compare with calypso as far as she was concerned.

Chad – Ebony's cousin who was staying with her family in East London – was long legged and bony. He lived in South London and thought East London was boring.

"I wish I was at home. I could be fishing now," he moaned.

"Well you're not, so stop going on about it.

You're getting on my nerves." Being sympathetic was not one of Ebony's good points.

"Well, you get on my nerves too," he retaliated.

Chad spent most of his time moping about, complaining about all the things he would like to do especially if it had anything to do with water. He moaned that being surrounded by girls made it worse for him, because they never wanted to do the things he wanted to do!

Ebony had another great love in her life and that was food. As long as it was edible she loved it. She wasn't fussy like Josette, her younger sister. Josette didn't like rice with peas in it, cake with currants in it or potatoes with eyes (but who does?). On the other hand, Helen, her elder sister, tried her hardest to resist food because she was frightened of putting on weight! Ebony was glad that her sisters were so stupid over food. She took full advantage and ate what they didn't want. Dinnertimes were a joy for her. Fried plantain, saltfish and ackee, or curried mutton and rice – you name it, she ate it.

Ebony was a little plump, but if she wasn't she wouldn't have been Ebony. Ebony's great-aunt Matilda who lived with her would sometimes say "You're as solid as a rock." This was a real compliment and Ebony would grin and reveal white, even teeth that had tackled many a plateful of good food.

Ebony was very conscious of her appearance, like most ten year olds. She loved the dresses her mother made. She used metres and metres of brightly coloured materials so that when Ebony spun round the dress would become "airborne" and reveal matching knickers. Even Ebony's socks were trimmed with the same material as the dress she was wearing for that day. With them she wore her Kicker boots.

Ebony's hair was mainly kept in plaits which were tied with ribbons made from the same material, but she had just begun to learn how to braid her own hair into a French plait at the back of her head. Ebony was very independent, unlike Josette who liked things done for her. But then Josette was only five!

Ebony could be a little forgetful sometimes, so her mother always made a matching bag to complete Ebony's outfit. She would wear this with the long handle across one shoulder and the bag at the front. Henry, her tiny teddy bear, would be attached to the handle by a ribbon. In the bag she would always have a couple of toffees, a tissue and her box of secrets. I can't tell you what was in it because it's secret!

From the start of the summer holidays Ebony had been learning to limbo which was proving to be very hard. She was trying to get under the broomstick which she had laid across two chairs in the dining room. Somehow she just couldn't get it together.

Her mother wasn't very happy that Ebony was trying to do this because she thought it was a little dangerous. But Ebony loved danger and so whenever her mother was out of the way she would have a go.

It was a bright, sunny morning in the middle of the week. Her mum was upstairs making the beds, so Ebony thought 'While the cat's away the mouse will play'. Out came the broomstick and across the chairs it went. Chad, who was fed up, sat watching Ebony struggling to limbo. He didn't help matters by jeering, "Ebony, your belly's in the way" or "Your head's too big." Then he would laugh out loud.

Ebony took no notice of him. She just carried on trying to limbo. And it wasn't long before she *did* do it – she managed to get under the broomstick without touching it!

She was jubilant. "I've done it, I've done it," she cried.

"How about doing it to music then? Let's see if you can do it," said Chad.

"Mum won't let me play my cassette down here, so how can I?"

"I know how." Chad proceeded to dig deep into his pockets. After pulling out a dirty hanky, a catapult and some sweet papers, he finally produced a bundle of soft tissue paper.

"What's that?" Ebony pointed to the package.

Grinning, Chad slowly unwrapped the paper. There in the middle of it was a miniature steel drum.

"Ohh," gasped Ebony. "A steel drum!" She reached out to touch it, but Chad pulled his hands back quickly. "No you don't. This is a very special steel drum and not for the likes of you to be touching."

"Where did you get it from?"

"That's my business."

"Hey," said Ebony. "Why don't you play it? Then I can do the limbo under the broomstick."

Staring at her as though she had grown two heads, Chad said "No".

"Why not?" pleaded Ebony. "Mum won't let me have my cassette down here, so playing your drum will be the next best thing."

You could see Chad's mind turning over and over. He looked down at the drum and back up at Ebony's wistful face.

"Please," whispered Ebony. She could sense that Chad wanted to play his drum. Perhaps if she was extra nice to him he would make up his mind in her favour.

"Hmm. You don't understand, Ebony," murmured Chad.

"Understand what?"

"This steel drum was given to my great-great-grandmother because she helped an old man when he was in trouble. The old man was really a king and because he loved helping people too he gave this drum to her. He said that if she played it and help was needed somewhere she would be transported to wherever it was."

"Oh, don't talk nonsense Chad, that sounds like a fairy story!"

"It's true. It is. But you only have forty-eight hours to help who or whatever needs you. Then you have to play the drum again to get back home."

Ebony folded her arms. She wasn't a fairy-story sort of person and she thought that Chad was stretching things much too far.

"I don't care what you believe, it is true. You can go and find someone else to play your music." Chad stood up ready to walk off. Ebony, realising her musician was deserting her, quickly changed her attitude. "Pleeeeaasse." Her large brown eyes and her hands clasped tightly together as though she was praying must have had an effect on Chad. After a breathless moment he said "Yes."

Overcome with joy, Ebony threw her arms around Chad's neck.

"Get off me!" he roared.

Quickly Ebony stood back, not wanting Chad to change his mind.

"Whenever you're ready," she said, standing by the broomstick.

Chad *was* ready. He began to beat out a tune that had Ebony throwing her arms and legs all over the place. Next, she was singing:

"Boom, boom, boom, boom I feel good
Boom, boom, boom, boom I knew I would
Boom, boom, boom, boom bending low
Boom, boom, boom, boom here I go."

Under the broomstick Ebony went. Once, twice, three times. Her eyes lit up like stars twinkling in the night. She was overjoyed. Chad was caught up in the electric atmosphere. He too began to dance around while playing his steel drum. Ebony started to dance with Chad and together they shook their shoulders and moved their bodies to the crazy beat. The music seemed to take on a life of its own. Ebony and Chad began to spin. First it was in time to the music, but then they spun faster and faster and faster until you couldn't tell which one was Ebony and which one was Chad. It seemed as though they were wrapped up together. They spun so fast that they bore a hole in the ground and disappeared through the floor.

They couldn't stop. They continued spinning, spinning down and down and down. They landed on what seemed like a soft mattress and bounced up again. The spinning stopped as they were flung apart. Breathlessly, they lay on their backs, panting and dizzy.

Everywhere was dim and dismal and very warm. Where were they?

CHAPTER 2

As their eyes quickly became used to their surroundings, they discovered that they were in some sort of forest. The trees were unusual shapes and colours – not tall and straight like normal trees, but bent and twisted. Some were very short. Some were dark red and some a mustardy sort of browny yellow. Others were a dark orange. Some were even covered in spots. There were no leaves on the trees, just a few twig-like branches. The trunks were gnarled and wrinkled – in fact they looked quite ill!

Ebony tried to stand up but it was impossible. The ground, which was a dark charcoal-grey colour, was softer and more springy than a mattress. It was as though lots and lots of grass had been cut and left lying around. It was difficult for her to walk, so she crawled on her hands and knees. Looking round for Chad, she found that he too was on his hands and knees.

"Where is it? Where is it?" he cried.

"Where is what?" asked Ebony.

"The steel drum. I've lost it."

"What do you mean, you've lost it? You had it in your hand a moment ago."

"Yes, I know. But that was when we were in the

dining room. Since we landed here, it's gone."

Ebony remembered what Chad had said about the story behind the playing of the drum. "Do you think we are on an adventure?" she asked excitedly.

"Where's my drum? It's too dark. I can't see a thing!" Chad wasn't listening to her.

"This is fantastic, a real adventure! I wonder where we are?" Ebony's mind was full of what might happen to them. "We could help to rescue the king's gold or kill some wild beasts or lead an army or …"

"Listen, if we don't find the drum we won't be going home … EVER!"

That brought Ebony back to reality. She didn't mind being away from home for a while, but going back was always nice – especially to sleep in your own bed. Then she thought about her dolls and teddy bears and her Mum's cooking. The two children began to paw the ground, desperately looking for the drum.

"Shh," said Ebony." "I can hear someone.'

Together they stopped moving and, straining their ears, they listened. Sure enough they heard, faintly, someone crying.

"Who's there?" called Chad who was a bit frightened.

"You're hurting us," said the voice in a soft whisper.

"Who?" Ebony was confused. "What do you mean, we're hurting you?"

"You're raking your fingers through us and it's painful. Please stop!" whimpered the voice.

"Where are you?"

"You're on top of us!"

Ebony and Chad realised that it was the soft ground which was talking to them. They sprang back, only to fall heavily on another spot of ground which groaned loudly. "Ugh!"

The ground rose up like a wave. Ebony and Chad were lifted up and down, like a boat bobbing on the water.

"The ground's talking!" squealed Chad. He tried to stand up, but couldn't.

"This is like playing in the water at the seaside," said Ebony.

"But how can the ground talk? I feel sick," groaned Chad, holding his stomach. "I wish it would stop moving."

"I wish you would stop complaining and start enjoying yourself. Yippee!" Ebony was thoroughly enjoying herself. She didn't forget her manners, however. Ebony apologised to the ground for hurting it and the ground moved the children nearer to the trees – in fact Chad bumped into one. "Ouch, you clumsy boy!"

Chad tried to throw himself back, but the ground was moving towards him and he bumped into the tree again. It howled, "Keep still!" so Chad lay on the ground at the base of the tree. The ground stopped moving and all was still.

"Wow, that was great fun! What happens now?" piped up Ebony.

"I want to find the drum and go straight home. I've had enough of this place."

"But why do you want to go home? You were bored there. Relax and let's enjoy this adventure!"

"It's boring."

"I'm fed up with you using that word. Everything's boring to you. Do you know what? *You're* boring."

"*I'm* boring?" said Chad, pointing a finger at himself. "You don't know how to have real fun. Anything pleases you."

The tree nearest to Ebony spoke to her haltingly as though speaking was difficult. "Put your hands ...around my trunk ...and pull yourself up." She wasn't at all surprised at the tree talking to her. If the grass could then why shouldn't the trees. Everything could probably talk! Hugging the tree tightly, Ebony was once again able to stand on her own two feet. "That's better. Why don't you do the same, Chad? Hold on to the tree and stand up."

Gripping the tree tightly, Chad slowly raised himself up. The tree kept complaining that he was either pinching it or digging his fingernails into its trunk. Chad finally stood up. Breathing slowly he said, "Ebony, we must find the drum. That's the most important thing right now."

Chad was holding on tightly to the trunk. His face was pressed against it. The ground around him seemed as though it was standing up and Chad yelled "Yeeeouch!" as something hit him quite violently on the back of the head.

Ebony squealed with laughter as something sailed through the air and hit Chad. "That should stop you moaning," she laughed.

Rubbing the back of his head, Chad seemed close to tears. "That wasn't funny. It hurt."

In the dimness of the forest Ebony looked over at Chad. There at his feet something sparkled. "Chad, what's that by your feet?"

"Where?"

"What do you mean where? By your feet, that's where. Look."

Hardly daring to turn round, Chad looked down at his feet. There was the steel drum.

"Hey, it's my drum!" He completely forgot that he needed to hold on to the tree. He let go and fell backwards. The ground moaned in pain. Rising up it threw Chad against the tree. The tree shouted out, "You stupid boy," and waving one of its branches it promptly smacked Chad on the leg.

"Ouch! What do you think you're doing?"

"Learn to stand still."

"It wasn't my fault, I was trying to pick …"

"Have you no manners, boy? Have you not learnt never to answer your elders back?"

"But you're not my elder." Chad kicked the tree. That was a wrong move because the ground lifted up and tossed Chad into the air. As he was coming down the tree caught him and tossed him up again and again.

Screaming with laughter Ebony began to clap in time to Chad's being tossed about. She started singing:

"Flying, flying in the air,

Look at Chad, he doesn't care.

Bouncing, bouncing all around –

That's until he hits the ground!"

And that's just what he did. As Chad landed on his hands and knees groaning, he said, "I'm going home now." He crawled over to the drum which was at the foot of the tree and picked it up.

"You're not going anywhere, young man," said the tree. "You were brought her for a purpose and until you have accomplished all that needs to be accomplished, you will never leave here."

Taking absolutely no notice, Chad began to play the drum. The thing about Chad was that he never listened and he never learned from his mistakes. The ground lifted up and tossed Chad once more. The drum fell out of his hand and rolled over to Ebony, who picked it up and put it in her bag.

"Now you can stop talking nonsense as you usually do, Chad, and let us get on with our adventure."

The ground stopped moving. Chad, weary and dizzy from being tossed up and down, slowly stood up with the aid of the tree trunk. "Do you realise we're prisoners, Ebony?"

Sighing, Ebony told him, "No we're not, we're here to help. Mr Tree was quite correct in saying that we are not leaving here until we have helped them. Just be quiet and let's find out what the problem is."

"Well said, young lady. Now we have sent for the Prime Minister who will be here shortly. He will explain everything to you." As the tree finished its sentence a squishing, rushing sound was heard.

"What's that?" enquired Ebony.

"That, my dear, is the Prime Minister and his entourage."

The noise grew louder and louder. Ebony looked at Chad, he looked at her and they were both thinking that perhaps this wasn't a good idea after all …

CHAPTER 3

The sound was deafening. Ebony and Chad had to cover their ears because it was so bad. The ground separated into a path that was coming nearer and nearer to them. Ebony squeezed her eyes shut. She thought that if it was something horrible she didn't want to see it.

"Greetings to you, children" said the voice very slowly. It sounded like great-aunt Matilda – but a bit lower – who came from the West Indies. "Welcome to the island of Merari, which is 1000 miles East and 1500 miles West and 1100 miles South and 2000 miles North of the nearest inhabited islands. It is usually summer all year round and we grow every conceivable fruit and vegetable, because of our lush climate. However, we are in unfortunate circumstances at present. We find ourselves trapped in this seasonal state – which is not a true season. That's why it hasn't got a name and nothing is growing. Furthermore you needn't be afraid of us so you can open your eyes."

At that, they both opened their eyes. There in front of them was a man, not much taller than them, with a large, wide feather at his back, towering over his head. He had a large moustache

that drooped down to his knees, and enormous bushy eyebrows. His brown skin looked as though it had shrunk in the wash. In fact all the people (and there was a crowd of them, roughly all the same height standing behind him) looked worn out and old.

"It's Uncle Rumus," exclaimed Chad.

"I'm sorry to disappoint you, young sir, but I am not your Uncle Rumus."

"But you sound just like him."

Stepping out from behind the Prime Minister (because that's who he was) came another man, even shorter. The man to whom you are speaking is the Left Honourable, His Most Gracious Fruitful and Overbearing Aginga Tobato Pomlagbomo," he said drawing in a deep breath.

"Thank you Tomroy. Now, down to business," said the Prime Minister (it's easier to call him that than his full title!) "If you young people would like to follow me I will take you to the Royal Residence and introduce you to the king," he yawned. His yawning was so contagious that everyone started to yawn – even the children.

"I don't want to meet the King, I want to go home and I demand to be set free to go home now," said Chad between yawns.

Another man stepped forward. He was the widest person that the children had ever met. It was like seeing three people in one – it wasn't fat, it was all solid muscle and tissue. Ebony thought he must have funny bones.

The man stood behind Chad. It was clear from this that Chad wasn't going anywhere, except to the Royal Residence. "We have ways of making you agree with our plans. Now come along. We have wasted time already."

The Prime Minister turned round and proceeded to go back the way he had come. The crowd turned round, too. Out in front were four little men. They might have been children, but Ebony thought it might be too impolite to ask. They had a giant broom which, instead of a brush, had a large roll of cotton wool at the end. As it was rolled, it cleared the ground and the dried grass blew away up into the air. The noise that it made was the dreadful sound the children had first heard, but it didn't seem so bad this time and they didn't have to cover up their ears.

"That's really clever," said Ebony, rubbing her eyes and trying to stifle the yawn that was trying to escape from her mouth. "By doing that you don't hurt the ground."

"Precisely," said the Prime Minister. "It is not our policy to cause unnecessary hurt or trauma to anyone or anything. That way we all get along famously."

They began moving along at a steady, slow pace through the forest. Ebony wanted to jaunt along as she walked and she was itching to start singing and dancing, but she didn't dare. The Prime Minister drew near to her and whispered, "If you feel like doing a song and dance please feel free to do so. Only I must warn you that we won't be able to join you as our happiness was stolen and we have nothing to sing and dance about, nor any energy to do it."

His words put a damper on Ebony's mood. She wondered how the Prime Minister knew she wanted to sing and dance. Filled with curiosity – even though she knew it was prying – she asked, "How was your happiness stolen?"

The Prime Minister burst into tears and so did the crowd behind him. As they were passing the trees, they too cried or wailed like a violent wind. The ground too began to heave and sigh and then it started weeping. The noise, together with the giant cottonwool broom, was louder than any noise you can imagine. It made Ebony's bones knock about inside, her blood turn cold, her head feel as heavy as lead and her ears pop.

The Prime Minister pulled out an enormous hanky and dabbed his eyes. He passed the hanky on to the next and so it went on around the crowd.

"Ugh! That's disgusting! How can you all use the

same hanky? You're passing on horrible germs. Yuck! It's terrible here. I want to go home." Chad's words stopped everyone in their tracks.

Breathing heavily, the Prime Minister turned to Chad and said, "On the Island of Merari we have no germs. In fact, we have no health problems, so sharing hankies is quite safe. And it will remain so unless you fail to help us."

That put Chad in his place. Everyone had stopped crying by now and the large hanky made its way back to the Prime Minister.

The pace quickened as the crowd surged forward. All of a sudden the Prime Minister stretched out his arms and said, "The Royal Residence of the Island of Merari."

Ebony and Chad couldn't see anything at first but soon, in the not too far distance, they spotted a large and impressive building. They were standing at the edge of the forest and in front of them was a town. The ground was covered with what seemed like sand, but it was the wrong colour – it was mauve! Ebony had thought that the forest was dark because most forests are. Now, standing on the edge of the town, she realised it was still dark. Peering up into the sky, she saw there was not a cloud in sight and the sky was a dark purple. It was all so odd. Ebony was trying to work out what was missing when the Prime Minister spoke up saying, "There is no sun and there never will be until our happiness is restored."

There were so many questions that Ebony wanted to ask him, but she knew that now wasn't the time.

As the crowd, with the Prime Minister and Ebony at its head, Chad behind them – and the wide man behind him – moved forward, people came out of their houses. They stood silently, watching the crowd walk through their town. No one cheered, no one smiled, no one spoke. It was as though they had been struck dumb and had all the stuffing knocked out of them.

Finally the crowd came to the forecourt of the Royal Residence, which on closer inspection was very shabby and not like a royal residence at all.

"It could do with a lick of paint," said Chad. (He was such an insensitive boy.)

The Prime Minister replied, "That, young man, is the least of my worries. All things will be restored to their former glory when what was once ours returns to our possession." Linking his arms through Ebony's and Chad's, he ushered them across the forecourt, up the steps and into the palace.

Inside it was even darker. It took a while for their eyes to get used to the dark.

"Why doesn't someone draw the curtains?"

inquired Chad.

"They are not closed. It's the lack of happiness that causes the darkness." The Prime Minister, with his arms still linked into theirs, led them through a series of corridors and up and down steps, stopping at a large door. He knocked three times quickly, three times slowly and then three times quickly again. The door opened slowly, creaking through lack of oil on its hinges. The Prime Minister stepped into the room and beckoned for the children to follow him. Ebony went first and gasped as she saw the King. He was well over two metres tall with a gigantic crown on his head that made him look twice his normal height. He had a thick mane of hair which fell to his broad shoulders. He too had a droopy moustache (I'm sure the Prime Minister copied him) but his brown skin wasn't shrivelled like everyone else they had met. He had the saddest eyes you could imagine. Ebony thought she saw a teardrop fall on to his cheek, but he wiped it so quickly she wondered if she was mistaken. There were a few brightly coloured, odd-shaped leaves inside glass jars dotted around the room. There were no light bulbs or candles and the faint light from the leaves gave the room an eerie kind of feel.

A woman, obviously the Queen because she too was wearing a crown, stood next to the King. She was shorter than the King but still tall – Chad thought that she would have been a good basketball player! Her crown was smaller than the king's, but it was still big! Ebony thought she was the most beautiful woman she had ever seen in her life (apart from her Mum). As Ebony looked closer, she was startled to see just how much the Queen did look like her Mum, but she was so much taller it couldn't be her.

The other thing that struck Ebony was the fact that the King and Queen looked a lot healthier than their subjects. 'Why was that?' she wondered.

"Come in, children," said the King. He held out his hands and motioned for them to sit in two enormous chairs. They were difficult to climb into, but Ebony and Chad had both experienced climbing over walls and trees and things like that so it wasn't long before they were both seated.

The Queen spoke. "May I begin by saying that when I first heard of your arrival I couldn't see how two young children could help us overcome our loss and bring about restoration. Now that I see you both I'm much encouraged and believe that you will be able to fulfil the task."

"Hmm, I don't want to appear to be rude, but what task is that?" yawned Ebony who wasn't one to mince her words.

"I'm not really interested in any task. I just want to go home," said Chad. He rudely stretched out his arms and opened his mouth so wide one would think he was catching flies!

"Oh, I see," said the Queen thoughtfully. "Haven't you told them, Prime Minister?"

Coughing, he mumbled something that the children did not quite catch. But the King and Queen did. They both stood up quickly. The Queen said, "Well, there's no time to lose. I can see already that you are both getting sleepy ..."

"You're right, Your Majesty. I feel as though I could go straight to bed," mumbled Chad. His mother would have been shocked at this because usually he was so reluctant to go to bed.

"Do you think we could have a sandwich, or better still a hamburger before we have a nap, please?" asked Ebony.

The King, Queen and the Prime Minister looked at each other and without words being spoken you could read their eyes and see the sorrow there. The Queen answered for them all. "Children, I don't know what a hamburger is or a sandwich, but I've a pretty good idea that it's food. I'm sorry to say we are unable to give you any but will you please listen to what I have to say?" Chad had nearly dropped off to sleep completely and Ebony was rubbing her eyes with one hand and her stomach with the other.

"Children, children," said the Queen quite loudly. "Please listen to me. You have to help us and soon. Already you are falling asleep, and that will not do. You have been called here for a purpose and it's very important that you accomplish it. Otherwise ..."

The Queen seemed lost for words at this point and the King continued. "Otherwise, you will be like us, trapped inside a dark world with no happiness, no brightness, everything dull and depressingly dark. No future." The King began to weep.

The sound of the King crying woke Ebony and Chad up. Ebony felt so sorry for him that she said, "Whatever you want us to do we will do it. You had better make it quick though, we have to be home within forty-eight hours of coming here."

That made Chad look at his watch. "And six hours have already gone by, and we only have ..."

He stopped to do some mental arithmetic but Ebony beat him to it. "That leaves forty-two hours. So what are we waiting for? Tell us what to do and let's be on our way!"

CHAPTER 4

The Prime Minister's speech began to pick up a little speed as he related to the children the dire situation that the Island of Merari was in. "Many, many years ago from an island that's a million miles away from here a young couple, Quako and Lydia, set out to start a new life. Both sets of parents were against the couple marrying and so when they did marry in secret it caused so much trouble that they decided to leave."

"Weren't their parents upset that they left?" asked Ebony.

"Of course they were, stupid. That's why Quako and Lydia had to leave in secret."

"Who are you calling stupid, stupid?"

"Now, now, children, we don't have a lot of time and quarrelling is such a waste." The Prime Minister continued his story. "Quako was a fisherman and he had heard stories that there were people who lived on other islands far away, but nobody had ever been there and returned to tell people about it. Lydia was so much in love with Quako that she was prepared to go to the moon and back just to be by his side.

"The couple stole away one moonlit night in

Quako's fishing boat. After many days and nights, they finally landed here. But years ago it was all forest and the couple despaired of ever clearing it and building a home and having children. Nevertheless, they chopped down a few trees and built a small house and they lived on fish from the sea. It wasn't long before they had a visitor, which came as a shock as they thought that they were the only ones who were on the island. This visitor was an old man whose name was Adonai and he was Lord over all the island."

Ebony, who had been pondering what was being said, asked, "Where did he come from?"

"Well, that's a question that many have asked but as yet there is no answer." The Prime Minister looked rather sternly at Ebony, before continuing. "Adonai told Quako and Lydia that he had been watching them and was impressed by their love for one another and how even though they had to chop down the trees and eat the animals and fish, he wanted to help them."

"But he was an old man. What could he do?" asked Chad.

"He was Lord over the whole island so he could do what he liked," cried Ebony who was growing a little impatient. She wanted to hear the end of the story and she felt the Prime Minister was taking too long.

"Perhaps I should take it up from here," said the King. "Now let's see. Adonai wasn't physically going to help them, but he helped them in a much better way. He gave them a very small plant ..."

"No it wasn't a plant," interrupted the Queen.

The King didn't look at all pleased at being interrupted. "A bush," he said quickly. "Adonai gave the couple a small bush. He told them to give it all the care and attention that they could, to love it like a baby and they would be surprised at the results. But once they had planted it, it must remain in the same spot, untroubled. If the bush was uprooted, the way of life that they would come to know would be taken away. Instead, a way of life that they hadn't known would come which would be most unpleasant – in fact, it may cost them their very lives."

"What was the bush like?" Chad was very interested in the story by now.

"The bush was like no other bush or plant or flower the couple had ever seen. Its brightly coloured leaves shone like the sun. The branches changed from silver to gold in the different seasons. Once the bush was planted it seemed to grow right before their eyes. The next morning they woke up to find some of the forest had been cleared and flowers and vegetables were growing. From that day on, the sun always shone and the island flourished and was very fruitful. Quako and Lydia thought of different names to call the bush and they decided to call it the Mookatook Bush. They had children and it became their job to watch over the bush and feed it loving attention. And for generations on this island, that is exactly what we have done."

"Don't tell me, don't tell me! I know what's happened," cried Chad, "someone's stolen the Mookatook bush and you want us to get it back for you."

"You're such a spoilsport, Chad. Why didn't you let the King finish it?" Ebony could see that the King was enjoying retelling the story about the Mookatook bush and now he looked sad again.

The Queen spoke. "You are right. That's why we need your help. Believe me, if we could bring it back ourselves, we wouldn't have waited this long for any help." She looked at the children and quickly added, "but we are so grateful that you have come and are willing to help us."

Ebony looked at Chad and if looks could change a boy into a frog he would have been croaking.

"Now, now," said the King. "We must make haste. Time is against us and you have far to go and a lot to do."

Ebony threw her arms into the air and yawned. "I need to eat and sleep first and then I'll be ready to do whatever it is you want me to do."

"I'm sorry, that's not possible. You see, the longer you stay here, the more sleepy you will become until finally you will become like our people. You will be unable to do anything."

Chad began to scratch. "But why?"

The Prime Minister spoke up. "Because the Mookatook bush gave us vitality and life. Without it we are like empty shells. Look, you are both sleepy and now you're scratching. That means that your skin will start to shrivel and then ..." he snapped his fingers, " ...you'll be like our people. So let's go." He began to tug both children by the arms and with the help of the King and Queen he got them to stand up.

"That's better," said the King. "I hereby appoint Ebony and Chad and the Prime Minister to the arduous task of locating the whereabouts of the Mookatook bush, capturing it and returning it to its rightful place." He took off his crown and placed it first on Ebony's head, then on Chad's and finally on the Prime Minister.

The Queen handed Ebony a box. Inside was a Mookatook leaf. "Guard this with your life. As you draw near to the bush, the leaf will begin to hum. It will shine so bright that you will not need to take it out of the box because the light will seep through. Please be careful and please hurry back."

By now the children could hardly keep awake,

and their skin was becoming dry and itchy. The Prime Minister was fully aware of the meaning of this so he held Ebony with his right hand and Chad with his left; with some force he led them out of the room, back through the palace and out into the forecourt.

Still leading them by the hand, he brought them to the back of the palace where the royal boats were kept. The royal servants had gathered to watch them – because of their lack of happiness and strength that was all they could do. The Prime Minister huffed and puffed, pushed and shoved the boat through the back gate and down towards the water's edge. He had to keep stopping to pull Ebony and Chad along as they were close to sleeping on their feet.

"Now we are ready," he said to the children. "Get in."

Clumsily Ebony got into the boat and lay down, fast asleep. Chad was more difficult. The Prime Minister nearly had to carry him into the boat because he was in a deep sleep. Chad flopped down, sleeping where he fell. Satisfied that everyone was on board, the Prime Minister turned and waved at the King and Queen who were at the window. They waved back. Slowly the waves moved the boat out to sea. The Prime Minister sat back and he too was nearly sleeping. The boat drifted further and further out into the middle of the sea.

It wasn't long before the boat began to pick up speed and tear through the waves. The spray from the water fell on the children and they woke up.

"Where are we?" asked Ebony.

"In the middle of the Merari Ocean, my dear."

Chad tried to stand up, but the Prime Minister told him it was best to sit down or he might fall into the sea.

"Where's the boat taking us?" he asked.

"To get the Mookatook bush back of course."

"Yes I realise that – but where?"

The Prime Minister became very serious and said, "To Great Ner, where we know the Mookatook bush was taken."

"How come you know where it is?" exclaimed Ebony.

"Because Taba and Saba were the two carers for the Mookatook bush when it was uprooted and stolen. Since then we have heard that they are in Great Ner living a life of luxury. They had been spying on us for ages and waited until the time was right to steal the bush and be long gone before we could get our hands on them. They were working for King Calaloo, a great enemy of ours."

Chad, who was only thinking about his own safety, asked, "Is the mission going to be dangerous?"

"In a word," the Prime Minister said, "yes."

Ebony and Chad sat silently thinking about what could lie ahead of them. The boat charged faster and faster across the water. Everyone held on tight to its sides. The speed was breathtaking. Ebony's eyes were popping out of her head as the water washed over her. From the end of the boat where Chad was sitting, a see-through hood began to rise up from the sides of the boat. It covered the boat completely.

"Wow, this is great," said Ebony.

"Why didn't the hood come up before? We wouldn't have got so wet," complained Chad as he tried to wring out his shirt. The Prime Minister didn't say a word. Suddenly the end of the boat rose up out of the water, causing Chad to fall on top of Ebony, who screamed out in pain. "You heavy lump! Get off!"

"It wasn't my fault."

The Prime Minister, gripping the boat tightly, said, "Hold on, children."

The boat plunged down into the water rapidly. Down, down, down it went, passing small shoals of fish, who looked at them in surprise. Down through the coral reefs it continued, until it reached the ocean bed. Then it skimmed even faster through the water, until everything was just a blur.

Chapter 5

POP, POP, POP went Ebony's and Chad's ears. The speed that the boat was travelling was immeasurable. It seemed as if the boat would keep flying along the ocean bed for ever. But at last the front of the boat reared up until it was back on top of the waves and slowing down. The hood peeled back revealing sunny blue skies. The boat seemed to have a mind of its own. It stopped at the edge of a sandy beach. There were palm trees in the background and along one side were big rocks covered in green moss.

The Prime Minister leapt out of the boat as though he had been given a new lease of life.

"Look, Chad, the Prime Minister's skin has changed!"

The Prime Minister, hearing Ebony, examined his hands and face. His eyes lit up and he gave a jump of joy. "Oh I feel like a new person, I've come alive. Hurrah!"

It was wonderful to see the instant transformation in him. His feather was standing tall and strong and his skin shone like a bright gold button. The children ran here and there as they too realised that they had regained all their lost energy.

"I'm starving and I really must have something to eat," wailed Ebony. It was most unusual for her to have gone without food for so long.

"First things first. We must hide the boat so that we will be able to get back home."

Together they pulled the boat behind the rocks. Chad climbed a tree and plucked off some of the palm branches. Ebony picked them up, took them back to the boat which the Prime Minister was securing and covered it up.

While they were all engaged in this, they were unaware that they were being watched. An old man was standing in the shade of the trees taking in all that they were doing.

When they had finished camouflaging the boat, they walked back towards the tree. They stopped. The man came out from the shadows of the trees and beckoned them. "Come quickly," he said.

The Prime Minister held out his hand to stop the children from moving forward. He wasn't sure if this man was friend or foe.

"Who are you?" he asked.

The man smiled. "There is no time for you to question me. Just trust me and you will have what you came here for."

Chad piped up, "How do you know what we came here for?"

"There is nothing that escapes my notice." He

continued to beckon them. "You must quickly eat and be refreshed because the time ahead is fraught with trouble. Hurry."

On hearing the mention of food, Ebony didn't wait. "I'm so hungry I could eat a horse. Where's the food?"

Chad followed Ebony and the Prime Minister moved slowly behind him. They walked in single file with the old man in the lead. He took them deeper and deeper into the forest, which seemed like a thick maze. He obviously knew where he was going because eventually he brought them to a hut. It was so well disguised in between the trees that they didn't see it at first.

"Welcome to my home," said the man.

The travellers trooped in. The hut was quite large and airy. The roof was thatched, with a hole to let the smoke from the fire out. There were onions and garlic hanging from the walls. Stacks of vegetables were in different parts of the room. There was a door at the back of the hut and Ebony wondered if that was where the bedroom was. There was a table with four chairs in the corner of the room. A plate piled high with bread and butter was waiting for them.

"Please sit," said the man. They didn't have to be told twice. Chad pounced on the bread and crammed a huge slice into his mouth. "Mmmmm.

This is delicious."

The Prime Minister, who was a great lover of food, ate two slices in about ten seconds!

The man brought over three plates on a tray and put them in front of them. On each plate were sweet potatoes, fish, patties, fried dumplings and plantain.

Minutes later, all the plates were clean and tummies were full. Then the man cleared away the plates and brought a mug of tea for the Prime Minister and two large glasses of strawberry milkshake for Ebony and Chad. When he had finished, Chad asked, "Where do we sleep?"

"Sleep? Sleep?" said the man. "There is no time to sleep, you have lots of work to do."

He cleared the table and produced a map. Pointing at various places on it he said, "I know all about you. I have planned out exactly what you should do and who you should meet to accomplish your mission and be successful."

"How do we know that you're on our side?" asked Chad.

"Of course he is, silly. He wouldn't have gone to all this trouble and know all about us unless he was on our side," replied Ebony.

"Correct, young lady. We have no time to lose. You will be entirely on your own except for the times you will meet up with the people I have alerted to look out for you. A word of warning ... if you don't stick to my instructions and the map, you will be doomed. Now go." He walked to the door and opened it. Looking out into the distance he pointed ahead. "That is the direction. Always look to the north-west side of the sun. Always remember these words:

Look to the sun that always shines,
Always keep this in your mind,
Never, never turn from the rock
And your way will not be blocked."

He made them repeat these words individually and then together as he showed them the rock whose peak touched the tip of the sun. The children thanked him as they went through the door. The Prime Minister was the last to leave. He shook the man's hand. "Thank you," he said.

The adventurers set off, filled with enthusiasm. All eyes were on the sun and the rock. Ebony turned to the Prime Minister and said, "We didn't even ask the man for his name. I wonder who he was?"

"That, my dear child, was the Lord Adonai."

"What?" shouted Ebony. "The Lord Adonai. How do you know?"

"Let's just say I know. He is just as eager for us to capture the Mookatook bush as we are."

"But why?"

Chad was fed up with Ebony asking so many

questions and he told her, "You really get on my nerves, Ebony. The Prime Minister has just told you why and yet you still have to ask a million questions. You didn't say a word to him while you were stuffing your face, did you?"

"I was not stuffing my face. You were, I saw you."

"You had no time to see me. Your eyes were only on your plate."

"Stop this now, children. Stop it."

They took no notice of the Prime Minister and continued to argue. They quarrelled so much that Ebony, who was in the lead, forgot all about the map Lord Adonai had given her and wandered off the route. They were all so angry with one another that they were totally unaware that the sun was no longer in front of them.

The forest had grown darker and it was difficult to see where they were going.

"Stop!" shouted the Prime Minister. At last, his shouting had an effect on the children. They finished arguing and stopped suddenly, remembering where they were. "We are now lost, thanks to you children. Give me the map," said the Prime Minister gruffly to Ebony.

"I'm sorry," she cried.

"It's a bit too late to be sorry. It's so dark I can't see properly." He moved ahead of Ebony, straining his eyes to see the map.

"Look, I think the best thing to do is to go back the way we came and start again. This is really terrible, to have only just started and be lost already. Now, no more arguing," he warned the children. "Follow me."

He turned but his way was blocked by a tree. As he tried to get round the tree, it moved. Chad tried to walk in front but another tree blocked his path. As he moved, the tree moved. Panic struck them. Stepping out from behind the trees were two men. One was tall, with a peanut-shaped head, from which his pointed ears stood out. The other man was round and fat.

"It's Taba and Saba," cried the Prime Minister.

"Oh no," wailed Ebony. "What shall we do?"

"Run," shouted the Prime Minister.

They ran and ran and ran. The ground was soft and mossy and they sprinted along with the Prime Minister breathing hard. All of a sudden the ground opened up and one by one they fell headlong into it.

Taba and Saba stood over the hole in the ground and laughed. "This has made our job all the easier. Goodbye, you interfering busybodies!" shouted Taba, as Saba waved goodbye to them.

"Come on," said Saba. "Let's get back to the palace and inform the King that we have successfully disposed of his enemies." With their arms round

each other, they jauntily walked off through the forest, happy with the fortunate turn of events.

CHAPTER 6

The pit was airless and very dark. It was difficult to stand up. They were floating almost as if they were in the swimming baths.

"I feel as though I've drunk too much wine," said the Prime Minister as he bounced around.

Never having had wine, the children couldn't agree with him, but they knew somehow what he meant. Ebony was having a great time. She flung herself up and down and around and about. "This is fantastic," she said.

"I feel sick," wailed Chad. "I want to stand up for just a minute and then I'll be all right." That wasn't to be. They continued to bounce around aimlessly.

Then a rush of cold air shot into the pit. At the same time the ground appeared from nowhere, causing them to bump into it.

"My head," moaned Chad. He sat rubbing it. Ebony had hit her knee and was rubbing that too. The Prime Minister had landed on his back and he wasn't at all pleased.

"Now what?" complained Chad. "How do we get out of here?" There was no door or window, just soil and bits of grass and twigs and things. Just then they heard a creaking sound like a door needing oil on its hinges.

A voice boomed out. "King Calaloo welcomes you to Great Ner. What a pity you won't be able to enjoy all that we have to offer. But such, I fear, is the hardship of going where you aren't wanted!"

His voice vibrated through Ebony's ears, which were still ringing even after he had finished speaking.

"What are you going to do with us?" The Prime Minister asked.

The voice laughed loud and long. "You have no need to worry. Now that you are here, you will soon see."

"Tell us who you are," said Ebony.

"I am the Keeper of the Dark. No one sees through me."

The creaking sound was heard again and the cold air turned hot. Soon it was baking. Chad took off his shirt and tied it round his waist. Ebony dug into her bag and brought out a tissue to fan herself. The Prime Minister stood up and fumbled his way along the walls. "There must be a way out of here," he muttered.

"No," boomed the voice.

The pit grew darker and darker. It was as though they were being suffocated.

"How can we get out?" wailed Chad. He *really* wanted to go home this time. The fun was over. This was serious. "Ebony," he said, looking at his watch, "Twelve hours have already gone by in our time. We are never going to get back home at this rate." Chad began to whimper. "I'll never see my mum and dad again."

"Stop it! Stop it!" shouted Ebony. "We can't give up at the first hurdle. We have to jump over it."

"How? How?" wailed Chad.

"Ebony is right of course," said the Prime Minister. "If there is a way into something, there surely must be a way out. Let's think."

They sat on the floor thinking, thinking. The minutes ticked by. Beads of sweat bubbled up on their foreheads and under their arms and dripped off the end of their noses, but they didn't let that deter them. Their lives were at stake.

The creaking returned and with it the voice. "I have orders from the King. He knows exactly why you are here. We heard you coming as soon as you set out. My job is to eliminate you unless …"

Ebony was quick off the mark. "Unless what?"

Laughingly, the voice said, "Unless you can get out of this dark prison."

"What do we need to do?" the Prime Minister asked.

"Find the key to fit the lock of the door."

Chad was frightened of the dark, so he was eager to be released from this dark, dank prison. "Quick, let's look for the door," he cried. He felt his way along the wall, searching in vain for the door. "It must be here somewhere."

"There's no point in looking for a door," the Prime Minister told Chad. "This is a riddle. We have to try and solve it."

The voice bellowed with laughter. "Yes. You are quite right. It's riddle time. Only that is the one thing you haven't got ...time. If you don't find the key to let you out within the next few minutes, you will remain there forever."

Jumping to her feet, Ebony said, "Listen, he keeps going on about a key to get out. We should be thinking about something that has to do with the situation we are in – not an *actual* key."

"Like what?" said Chad.

"Well, like the opposite of being underground is being overhead."

"Oh I see," said Chad. "Hmm." He began to think. "Because it's hot, cold?"

"That's right, Chad. Keep thinking like that."

They came up with all sorts of things. The Prime Minister said, "Prison and bars?" That didn't go down too well.

"Light!" shouted Ebony. This was so obvious that it was the last thing they thought of. At that word, the pit wasn't so hot and dark.

"Can you sense a change?" whispered Ebony.

Sure enough they did.

"You'll never get out," said the voice, which didn't sound as menacing as it did before.

They all shouted at the top of their voices, "Light, light, light." The temperature began to fall.

"There's something missing," said the Prime Minister. "We haven't quite got there, yet."

"What we need is some real light," said Chad. "But where can we get it from? None of us have a torch."

"I know," screamed Ebony with delight. She delved into her bag and carefully brought out her secrets box. No one could see what she was doing. Ebony couldn't either, but she knew what she wanted.

Quickly her hands groped round the box and held it up. A flare of light burst into the darkness. It was the box that held the Mookatook leaf. This was the light.

Instantly their dark prison was flooded with a bright light that forced the darkness back. The roof of their prison opened to reveal blue skies once again. The voice ranted and raved and screamed and shouted at them but the ground rose up and, when they were level with the grass, they ran towards the sun.

"We're free, we're free!" shouted Chad with delight. They kept running. The Prime Minister was trying to keep up with the children. He was waving the map in his hand. "Children, children, stop a moment," he cried. But they were so glad to be free they continued running and running. The problem for the Prime Minister was that instead of getting out of breath, it seemed that they were getting stronger. It was difficult for him to stop them.

The forest cleared. In front of them was a large lake. Around the lake were people who were either swimming or fishing or just lazing around soaking up the sun.

A little girl with thick black curly hair, large brown eyes and skin that shone like a shiny penny came up to them and said, "My name is Nina. Welcome. This place is called Temptonier and we are called Tempters. It is filled with beautiful things. Come and enjoy yourselves."

The children were excited. They gave no thought to their plans for finding the Mookatook bush, let alone following the map. After coming out of their dark prison, they had truly found paradise.

CHAPTER 7

"I think we should hold a conference," said the Prime Minister to the children. He sensed that all was not well here and he wanted to warn Ebony and Chad before they got too involved. He suspected that this was another ploy to stop them from getting the Mookatook bush from King Calaloo.

"I'm going to have a swim," shouted Chad as he raced across to the lake, stripping off his trousers and leaving his shorts on. They watched as he plunged into the lake.

"It's great in here. Why don't you both join me?" he called.

"I think we should have a word first, Chad, and then we can enjoy ourselves," said the Prime Minister. His words fell on water-clogged ears – Chad was too busy swimming. Turning to Ebony, the Prime Minister was just about to talk to her about Chad when they heard music. It was calypso. To the right of them a group of Tempters had set up their instruments and had started to play. Ebony didn't stop to think twice. Already a group of people were dancing. Ebony rushed up to the centre of the group and began to dance. Oh how she danced! Her eyes were bright and her cheeks glowed with

pleasure. This was the life. Some of the men brought out a pole which they laid across two tree stumps. Ebony didn't wait to be asked before she was limbo-ing underneath it. She lost count of how many times she managed to go beneath the stick without touching it and still dancing to the music.

All this time the Prime Minister was worried. He didn't know what to do. Chad was by now climbing up a rock and diving into the lake. Ebony appeared to be totally caught up with the music.

He sat down and thought, 'What can I do?' He kept looking round for a way of getting Chad and Ebony away from the Tempters. He just couldn't think. The Prime Minister felt such a failure. Time was running out and getting the Mookatook bush back seemed more impossible than ever. With downcast eyes he whispered, "I've failed the King and Queen and the whole of my country." He looked at the map and thought he might as well tear it up and throw the remains away. "What's the use?" he cried.

Then he thought he would study the map just once more before getting rid of it. Peering at the paper he located with his finger where they were. Turning the map round he realised that they were not too far off course from where they were supposed to be heading. A flicker of hope and a bit of determination came into his mind. "Now, how can I lure the children back?"

He was more convinced than ever that these people had been instructed by King Calaloo to waylay them if Taba and Saba failed. And then perhaps to get rid of the three of them. It seemed so unbelievable because Ebony and Chad were having so much fun.

Chad was climbing up a steep rock and diving into the water like an expert (which he certainly wasn't). The people around him kept encouraging him to do it again and again. And that's what he did. He seemed to be growing tired, but with the folks around him urging him more and more he couldn't stop himself. The Prime Minister walked quickly over to Chad as he came out of the water.

"Chad, don't you think you should stop this? You're looking tired."

A young man stepped in front of Chad and, placing his arm round Chad's shoulders, answered for him. "He's doing fine. He's got a lot of life in him yet."

Chad was finding it difficult to catch his breath. He just gave the Prime Minister a watery grin and walked off slowly towards the rock.

Meanwhile Ebony was also showing signs of tiredness but the music, which was getting louder and louder, continued to hypnotise her. Some of the women surrounding her kept pulling her this way and that – not even giving Ebony a moment to rest.

All the while, they told her what a good dancer she was. Ebony, being Ebony, had to live up to all the praises she was receiving.

The more the Prime Minister looked round the more he could sense "unseen" eyes watching as they were being sucked into a sinister plot to delay them from moving on.

Just then, Nina came to him and said, "My father has been watching you. He says would you like to join him for lunch and a glass of wine."

The Prime Minister was on the alert. How did these people know that his weakness was food? They had caught Chad with water and had hypnotised Ebony with calypso music. Now they wanted him and they were trying to get him through his stomach. He wasn't having any of their tricks.

"That would be nice," he said. "I think the children would like something to eat too."

Nina was unaware that the Prime Minister had realised their wicked intentions and so she rushed over to Chad and told him to stop swimming and come and have some lunch. Then she ran over to Ebony and invited her to eat too.

Nina's father's house was very large, made of dry grass and stones with foundations built on stilts. The trio were invited to sit round the long table that was loaded down with food. Ebony and Chad feasted their eyes. There was a gigantic black forest gateau, an enormous plate filled with fresh mangoes and starfruit. Ham, corned beef, cheese and pickle sandwiches and pieces of coconut cake were piled high on plates. Bottles of fizzy drinks of every flavour and colour and jugs of fruit juice were lining the table at one side. A big fish, which looked as though it had been roasted over a spit, dominated one end of the table and a pyramid of fruit and vegetables the other. Coconut drops and nut crunchies, all sweet and sticky, were next to a plate of jam tarts. One of Ebony's favourites, ackee and saltfish, was standing next to a plate of rice. Ebony made a beeline for that. "My favourite," she squealed.

While Ebony had been dancing and Chad had been swimming, the Prime Minister had been very strong and tried to encourage them to stop what they were doing – because he had not been exposed to temptation. Now he was being tempted by food, which he loved so much that his resistance was growing weak.

"Hmm, maybe just a sandwich or two," he said as his mouth began to water and his stomach juices started to churn. He stepped tentatively towards the table, hands outstretched and ready to grab the nearest plate to him.

"No, wait!" shouted Ebony. She seemed to regain

her senses. "*Look to the sun that always shines.* Which direction is that?"

Those words were like a rap on the head for the Prime Minister. "Thank goodness. I was nearly done for."

"Please eat up," said Nina. "My father will be here soon and he will be most disappointed if you haven't eaten anything."

"To be truthful, I don't feel hungry any more," said Ebony with one eye on the food-laden table.

A young girl, not much older than Nina, hurriedly picked up the plate of ackee and saltfish and held it under Ebony's nose. She only said one word: "Eat."

Shuddering, Ebony tried to resist the food. The Prime Minister threw out his arm and knocked the plate to the floor.

"What a waste," said Chad. "I'm starving and I'm going to eat some of everything."

"Oh no you're not," said Ebony, holding on to Chad's arm.

"Oh yes I am, and nobody – especially you – is going to stop me."

The Prime Minister quickly held on to Chad's other arm, saying, "I think it's time we left."

Ebony and the Prime Minister tried to get Chad out of the house before he ate any food. It proved to be very difficult.

When they reached the door a large man with a beard right down to his ankles blocked the way. "Hah, our guests. Are you leaving?"

"Yes," said Ebony. "We have an important assignment and we must go now."

"I'm hungry," growled Chad.

Ebony kicked him on the ankle.

"Well, I think this young man deserves some food before you leave. Let him eat."

"That's not possible because as Ebony has said we really must be going," replied the Prime Minister.

"Not until you have all eaten."

People had now gathered around the trio, boxing them in on all sides. Defeated, they slowly turned back into the house.

"Now, isn't it better that you co-operate with us? And look at all this food we have prepared for you." Nina's father held up his hands. "Before you eat a morsel, we would like to offer you our speciality."

A young girl and boy came through the door at the back. The boy held a large glass jug with a blue-green liquid in it and the girl carried a tray with three glasses. "Please drink this elixir whose ingredients will grant your heart's desire."

"No thanks," said Ebony.

"Nothing for me either," said the Prime Minister who suspected that the drink contained something that would severely affect them for the worse. He was right.

Nina, her father, the pair who held the glasses and the jug of drink and the rest of the household stood around the trio. Their faces were stern – all except Nina who said in a very gentle voice, "This is a very nice drink. It will do you the world of good. Please drink it." The boy poured the drink into the glasses and the girl handed one to each of them.

Ebony definitely didn't want hers and said so. No one took any notice of her. The Prime Minister gingerly held his glass. Chad had somehow come to his senses by this time. He said demandingly, "We don't want this drink and nothing you can do will make us have any. Furthermore we want to leave." Ebony had never seen Chad so courageous.

Nina's father said, close to Chad's ear, "Take my advice young man …" and then very loudly, "Drink!"

Such an order might have given Chad no choice. But no, he leapt to his feet and shouted back, "If you're so concerned about me drinking this stuff, why don't you have some too?" He threw the contents of his glass over Nina's father.

The Tempters gasped in horror, as did Ebony and Chad and the Prime Minister. As soon as the liquid touched Nina's father, there was a hiss and a puff of smoke. As the coloured liquid ran slowly down his face and over his body, he began to turn a bluish-green. Then he started to dissolve into a jelly-like substance. His face began to disappear into his neck, his neck into his shoulders and his shoulders into his chest. Soon he was just a large jelly-like mess on the floor.

The room exploded into confusion. Ebony and the Prime Minister threw the contents of their glasses over the people standing nearest to them and the same thing happened – they began to dissolve. Chad grabbed the jug with the remaining liquid and began to toss it round the room and as it landed on people they too dissolved. The floor became sticky with everyone melting around them.

"Quick, we had better make ourselves scarce," said Chad. He took hold of Ebony's hand. She grabbed hold of the Prime Minister's and together they fled.

Down the steps of the house they ran, past the place where Ebony had danced and by the rocks where Chad had dived (he picked up his clothes on the way). They raced along the beach, not stopping to look behind at the angry Tempters who were pursuing them. They needed all their strength to get away. It seemed that the harder they ran the more the Tempters were gaining on them. The sandy beach beneath their feet began to pop up in lumps and bumps.

"What's happening now?" thought Ebony. "What else can go wrong?" Little did they know it but what was now happening meant they were getting help!

From under the sand, crabs of all sizes emerged and three of the largest ones appeared just in front of Ebony, Chad and the Prime Minister.

"Hop on," the crabs cried. The group didn't think twice. They leapt on to the backs of those crabs and away they sped.

CHAPTER 8

The crabs ran faster and faster. Ebony, with arms outstretched, had to keep pulling her dress from her face because it kept blowing over her. Chad found it easier to crouch down and hold on to the back of his crab, while the Prime Minister was grasping tightly to the sides of his crab's shell. He was sitting backwards – which was a little dangerous!

Soon the Tempters were a blob in the background. They hadn't been able to keep up with the mighty crabs. The crabs gently slowed down, until they eventually stopped. The trio were quite weary by this time. Wobbling on her legs, Ebony said, "Where are we?"

Her words made Chad and the Prime Minister look around. They were in a desert. Nothing but sand and more sand for miles around.

"What do we do now?" said Chad.

One of the crabs responded to his question. "I guess you will have to follow the map. Cheerio." Before anyone could say another word, the crabs disappeared under the sand in less than a second. Soon the surface was smooth and flat. If it wasn't for the fact that they had seen the crabs disappear with their own eyes, they would have never believed that there had been crabs at all!

The Prime Minister, happy that he hadn't destroyed the map, pulled it out from his pockets. "Now then, the crab was perfectly right in what it said. If we had stuck diligently to the map we wouldn't be in this mess."

Chad became very indignant. "I hope you're not blaming me. I ..."

"Yes I am blaming you. If you hadn't gone charging off into the water, we could have missed out on all that aggravation."

Ebony began to snigger.

"And as for you, young lady, you're just as much to blame with all that dancing. You didn't stop to think about the mission we are on – you were just intent on pleasing yourself."

Both children stood in front of the Prime Minister, hanging their heads in shame. The King and Queen had given them a very important task, one that would have dire effects on the country if they didn't fulfil it and they had been pleasing themselves. They knew they deserved the rebuke.

"Now," continued the Prime Minister, taking a little glass bottle containing sand from his pocket. "From my calculations, nearly twenty-eight hours have gone." He shook his head.

"Twenty-eight hours!" exclaimed Ebony. "We had better get a move on."

"A move on where? What do we have to do?" said Chad.

The Prime Minister bent down and looked at the map and the two children knelt either side of him. The Prime Minister twisted the map this way and that, upside down and round and about. He *ohhhh*ed and *ahhhh*ed and grunted and moaned

"Are we lost?" asked Chad.

"Hmm ...well ...I ..."

"We're lost," said Ebony. "Here, let me have a look Prime Minister." His face fell. He hated having to give something up that he couldn't work out. To soften the blow, Ebony said to them, "Why don't you both try and remember what Lord Adonai said?"

Eager to be useful, the Prime Minister jumped at the chance to prove his worth. "Okay Chad, let's show Ebony that we can do it. Right. The first line went: *Looking at the sun, shining in the sky.*"

"No it didn't. It went: *Look to the sun that always shines.* Think about it."

"Ah, I think the first bit is right, but I don't remember the *think about it* bit."

"Yes it did. It definitely said *think about it.* I'm very good at remembering things, you know."

"Well, this time I'm very sure you're wrong. *Look to the sun that always shines* ...and ...and ..." He began to scratch his head.

Luckily for them Ebony had found their position on the map. "Here we are."

Chad and the Prime Minister both heaved a sigh of relief. Neither of them could remember the words.

"This is where we are," she pointed to a yellow area on the map. "Now this is where Great Ner is, so I don't think that we are very very *very* far away, just perhaps very very far away."

"In other words, we have a bit of a way to go then," said Chad yawning.

"Yes, it looks that way. Oh, did you both remember the words?" Chad and the Prime Minister looked at each other. No one said anything.

"I suppose that means no." Opening her bag, Ebony took out a piece of paper. "It's a good thing that one of us has some sense, otherwise we'd all be doomed." In a clear voice she said:

"Look to the sun that always shines,
Always keep this in your mind,
Never, never turn from the rock
And your way will not be blocked."

"You've had that all the time and you made us try to remember," cried Chad, very put out.

"I had to because I needed to study the map and if we had tried to do it together we wouldn't have agreed."

"Very sensible, very sensible," said the Prime Minister, obviously pleased with Ebony.

"Okay," said Ebony, basking in the Prime Minister's praises. "Here we are in the middle of a desert, surrounded by sun – so that's the first part of the rhyme. Where's the rock?"

Standing with their backs to each other and their hands shielding their eyes from the rays of the sun, they each looked for the rock.

"There it is," pointed the Prime Minister. "It's quite a distance away," he added sadly.

"We had better get started then," said Ebony,

folding up the map and putting it into her bag.

Dragging his feet, the Prime Minister said softly, "I think we had better face the fact that we haven't got enough time to get the Mookatook bush and be home before your forty-eight hours are up." He was on the point of tears.

"You're right, Prime Minister. I think we should forget all about the Mookatook bush and King Calaloo and head for home, Ebony."

"You would think that, Chad, but I think that if we keep going we may do it. My Mum always says, if at first you don't succeed, try, try and try again."

Brightening up a little, the Prime Minister replied, "I think your mother is a very clever woman, Ebony, and so is her daughter."

Ebony's smile dazzled the Prime Minister so much he had to shield his face with his hands.

"I'm tired, I need to go to sleep and I'm starving too," said Chad.

"Here, have a toffee," offered Ebony.

"What's a toffee going to do? It's ages since we've eaten and having a toffee will only make me more hungry."

"Thank you very much, dear," said the Prime Minister gratefully. Quickly undoing the wrapper he popped the toffee into his mouth. Ebony did the same with hers and Chad, not wanting to be left out, held out his hand too. "I thought you didn't want one?"

"I can change my mind, can't I?"

Chewing the toffee kept them silent for a while. The desert seemed endless, the rock was still a speck in the distance and secretly Ebony was thinking that the Prime Minister was right – they might not make it in the remaining twenty hours. She tried not to dwell on the negative side of the situation. Instead, linking her arm through the Prime Minister's, she plodded on.

The sun began to sink down behind the rock and darkness was creeping up on them. They were all very tired, not having slept for a very long time and, what with heat and all the running and dancing and swimming and everything else that they had done, they were near collapse.

"Excuse me," said a voice behind them.

They all jumped and, turning round, saw a very tall man. He was the thinnest man they had ever seen. His legs were like broomsticks, his hands were like twiglets and he had thick black hair that hung down his back in plaits.

"You're all on your way to the King of Great Ner's palace, I take it?"

"How do you know?" said Ebony, astonished.

Smiling, the man held out his long, thin arms and said, "Malu Walla's the name. I've been tracking you for a bit and ..."

"Are you a friend of Lord Adonai's?" asked the Prime Minister.

Grinning from ear to ear, Malu said, "You've got it in one. I suppose you'll be needing somewhere to sleep and something to eat?"

"I'm starving. What have you got?" said Chad. He really was a selfish boy.

"Let's see."

Not giving Malu a chance, Chad continued, "By the way, Malu, where are we going to sleep? Surely not in the middle of a desert?"

Bending over and looking Chad right between the eyes, Malu said, "Where else were you planning to lay your head down tonight, little boy?

CHAPTER 9

"What about the wild animals?" asked Chad. He was a bit frightened.

"What about them?" said Malu. "If we get eaten that's the end of that, or should I say, that's the end of us so there's no point in worrying."

The Prime Minister felt he had to say something reassuring. "Well, I'm sure everything will be all right, Chad, because if Lord Adonai has sent Malu to look after us, things will turn out well."

"But," continued Chad, "can Lord Adonai protect us from mad, hungry, wild animals? That's all I want to know."

"Put it this way Chad: can we protect ourselves? No. So stop moaning and let's get ourselves settled for the night." Looking around, Ebony was wondering how that was going to happen. She needn't have worried. Malu had a medium-sized bag on his back which he took off and put on the ground. Opening it, he pulled out a rather tough type of brown sacking.

"Grab hold of this will you, please?" said Malu. Between the Prime Minister and Chad they pulled and pulled the sacking out of the bag. All three of them were amazed at the amount that came out.

They were surprised that it fitted into the bag in the first place.

Unzipping a side pocket, Malu took out some wooden pegs and a hammer. "Put the tent up will you?" he said to the Prime Minister and Chad. What a mess they made of that! They turned the sacking (which was a tent) this way and that. They were finally engulfed by it.

"Get me out," shouted Chad.

"Wait a second, boy. Hold this," said the Prime Minister.

Ebony looked at Malu and he grinned. "That will keep them busy for a while. Could you help me cook our supper, Ebony?"

She didn't have to be asked twice – anything to do with food was a pleasure and not a chore for Ebony.

Out of the same bag which Ebony reasoned must be a bag of miracles or something of that nature, Malu took a camp stove and a plastic tub. In the tub was a loaf of bread, some cooking oil, a tin of beans, some odd-looking vegetables which could have been a type of wild grass and chunks of meat. There were other bottles and tins and packets that Malu took out of the bag. Even before some of the things were cooked the smell triggered off Ebony's appetite. If Malu had said that they could have been eaten as they were, she wouldn't have hesitated.

Malu snapped his fingers and the stove was lit. It wasn't long before the food was sizzling in a pan. Ebony had buttered half the loaf of bread and made a pot of tea. Malu also had a few packets of milky drinking chocolate, which Ebony loved (she didn't drink tea, neither did Chad).

When the meal was completely ready, Malu rescued the Prime Minister and Chad. He disentangled them from the tent.

Breathing freely again, the Prime Minister was relieved to be out in the open air. As for Chad, he was just about to complain that there was something wrong with the tent when he spied the plates piled high with food. "I'm starving. That looks great."

Malu held out his arm and told Chad that he had to wait until everything was ready before he ate.

"Is there anything else to cook?" said Ebony.

Shaking his head, Malu plunged into his bag and took out a small folding table and matching chairs. "Please sit down." He waved his arm across the table on which Ebony had placed all the plates, the teapot and the mugs of chocolate. "Enjoy yourselves."

"Aren't you having a bite to eat, sir?" asked the Prime Minister.

"Please, don't think of me, eat your fill."

Malu didn't have to repeat himself. They tucked ravenously into their meal. By the time they had finished, Malu had erected the tent, which was on wheels – most unusual. He had also set up a lamp and had got a fire going. Not too far away to the left of the tent, he had put up some screens. "Here is your bathroom," he said.

"Bathroom!" squealed Ebony. "I haven't had a bath for …" she had to think a minute " …for about two days."

"You can go first then," said Chad. "You will need a bath more than me." (Chad was not one for bathing even though he loved water!)

So while Ebony was bathing and getting ready for bed, Chad and the Prime Minister helped Malu to wash the dishes, pots and pans and put them all back into his miraculous bag.

Inside the tent, they had their own sleeping bag. There was enough space for them to stretch and toss and turn quite easily. Malu popped his head into the tent. "Everything all right in here, folks?"

"Yes, thank you," was the chorus of replies.

"Goodnight."

Sleepily they all said goodnight. Malu put the lamplight out and darkness fell on the tent. "He's a decent sort of chap, isn't he?" whispered the Prime Minister.

Yawning, Ebony mumbled something that the Prime Minister couldn't catch, so he said to Chad, "What did she say?"

Chad mumbled, "Ididn'thearherproperly." This

sounded like gobbledegook to the Prime Minister, so he said "Goodnight, children. Sleep well. We have a long journey ahead of us tomorroooooow." He snored.

They slept through the whole night. Even if they had been attacked by wild animals they would have slept all the way through it. They could have been attacked in their beds, but their defence would have been snores which wouldn't have frightened anyone. As it was, they were protected by Malu.

Throughout the whole night, after packing away the bathroom and all the equipment he had used, he harnessed himself to the tent and pulled the sleeping trio across the desert. Even though Malu was as skinny as a beanpole, he had the strength of fifty men. He pulled the tent over the hills and through the valleys. All the while, his eyes – which had been trained to see in the dark – were kept on the rock. He never turned to the left or the right, he just kept plodding on.

It was midday when the Prime Minister awoke. He had had such a wonderful sleep. He had dreamt of the Mookatook bush being replanted in its rightful place, and the King and Queen looking at him in deep gratitude and the people of Merari proclaiming him to be the best Prime Minister that they had ever had. Waking up and finding himself in a sleeping bag in a tent brought him back down

to earth with a bump. Rolling over, he tried to get out of the bag. It was difficult.

"Malu, Malu," he called. "Do you think you could give me a hand? I can't seem to get out of this tiresome thing."

There was no reply. Rolling over, he prodded Chad. "Wake up, boy." Sleepily, Chad pushed him away. First thing in the morning Chad was terrible. It took his mother ages to turf him out of bed, when only the night before it had taken ages to get him into it! This day was no different.

Not meeting with much success, the Prime Minister rolled back again and shook Ebony. "Good morning, dear. Rise and shine. Do you think you could give me a hand with this sleeping bag? It seems to have a life of its own – I can't get out of it."

Ebony yawned, rolled over and climbed out of her sleeping bag. She had a smile on her face. "Good morning, Prime Minister. What's the problem?"

He told her what the problem was. Ebony really was a helpful child. She was the complete opposite to Chad in the mornings and it was a pleasure to be in her company. Kneeling down, she tugged at the zip of the bag. Within a moment, she had freed the Prime Minister.

"I'm so grateful to you, dear. That boy really is the most miserable of creatures."

"Yes, I know," said Ebony. She would have said a lot more but the Prime Minister asked her to find out what had happened to Malu. He had called him, but there was no reply.

Opening up the flap of the tent, Ebony peered outside. She gasped and darted back into the tent again. Then slowly she approached the flap again and gingerly looked out.

"Goodness me," she said. "Oh dear."

"What's the matter, Ebony?" said the Prime Minister, struggling to stand up. His bones were a bit stiff, he needed some oiling, he thought.

"You had better have a look." She stood back, still holding the flap, to let the Prime Minister look out.

"Upon my word," he gasped in utter surprise.

Chad had woken up by now, the last as usual. "What's happened?"

"You had better come and have a look, young man. We now have to figure out how to get through this lot."

Scrambling out of his sleeping bag, Chad pushed the Prime Minister none too gently aside and looked out.

"Oh no," he wailed. "I want to go home, and I mean it this time!"

CHAPTER 10

"Malu, Malu!" they called. But it seemed as though Malu had disappeared. "He seemed like a really nice man. How could he bring us to this place? We're well and truly lost now," moaned Chad. "Come on, Ebony, give me the steel drum. We're going home right now, I've had enough."

"I've had enough of you!" shouted Ebony. "All you do is moan and groan and complain and think about yourself. Look how far we have come and still you're not happy." Pointing her finger at him – even though her mother had said that was a rude thing to do – she continued, "When we get home – and I said *when* – if I ever hear you complain about a single thing I'll ... I'll ..."

"You'll what? You can't do a thing to me that I couldn't do to you and worse. Look at you. You're just a little girl and ..."

Wearily the Prime Minister held up his hands. "Children, children. This is not the time to be squabbling. We have a major task ahead of us. We must get ourselves out of this mess, reach Great Ner, find the Mookatook bush and get back home again. We are wasting very precious time. Now stop this at once."

And they did, looking somewhat remorseful.

"Right, now we have you two sorted out, how are we going to deal with *this*?" He pointed his finger.

In front of them was a forest, but the trees looked most odd. They were not too tall, but tall enough. They were square in shape and the leaves were sharply pointed. The leaves grew from leg height, which meant they would tear at their faces, arms and the upper part of their bodies.

The Prime Minister stretched out his hands from the tent and plucked one of the leaves. It was sharp and he pricked his finger. "Ouch!" he screamed. "These leaves are very dangerous. How are we going to get through this?"

"Why did Malu bring us here in the first place? I thought he was on our side," said Ebony.

Sitting on his sleeping bag, Chad said, "I knew that man had a funny look in his eye, but you wouldn't have listened to me. Now look at the mess he has got us into."

Ebony wanted to cry. This really was tough. Taking the map out of her bag, she held back the tears as her finger traced the distance they had come. There was still some way to go before they reached the palace of Great Ner.

The Prime Minister sat down and took out his red handkerchief. Dabbing his eyes, he felt like a failure. No more would he see Merari. This was the end of the road for him.

A cloud of depression hovered over the travellers. How were they going to get through that deadly forest of thorns? They all sensed the hopelessness of the situation.

Chad was thinking about being at home and eating his mother's food. He was fed up with all this adventure business – especially when he was in the company of an old man and a little girl. Now if he had been with his friends, that would have been another story. They would have had a lot more fun.

Going home was the last thing on Ebony's mind. She did miss her family and sleeping in her own bed but it wasn't every day that you had an adventure. When she finally got home (and she dreaded to think what her parents were doing, since she and Chad had been missing), she would be able to relate how she had taken part in restoring the Mookatook bush to its rightful owners. That all seemed like a dream now. Surely, there must be a way that she could get them out of this mess?

Suddenly she jumped up. "Guess what?" she cried. The others turned to her, startled at her outburst. "Malu hasn't lost us. He has brought us to the right place!"

"That can't be right," said the Prime Minister.

"Well, look at the map then." She held out the map for the Prime Minister to see.

It only took him a moment to realise that what Ebony said was true. "You're quite right, my dear. We *are* in the right place. But how on earth do we get through?"

Filled with renewed hope and vigour, Ebony went through the flap in the tent and stood facing the forest. The Prime Minister and Chad were close behind her.

"I'm not going through that prickly forest to be cut to ribbons, so you can forget that," complained Chad.

Ebony murmured to herself, "We need something to help us cut a path through it. Hmm." She pondered on the problem.

"We need an axe, that will do the job," the Prime Minister said.

Mockingly, Chad replied, "An axe? You mean a pneumatic saw!"

"What's that you say, Chad? A pneumax something or other?" said the Prime Minister.

"One of these things." Chad held out his hands, waved them in the air and made loud humming noises. "One of these."

"I don't recall seeing anything of that nature. You say it would chop down the forest? Sounds remarkable indeed."

"Nothing else is going to cut that lot down without doing ourselves a lot of harm." Chad sat down outside the tent with his arms folded. He was pleased in a way. Maybe this problem, which wasn't going to be solved easily, would make Ebony realise that they had better go home. He smirked slyly.

"I've got it," shouted Ebony happily. She had opened her bag and was holding up a miniature pair of scissors.

Chad burst out laughing. "Ebony," he guffawed. "You really think," he rolled over with laughter " ...that you will cut down ..." tears were running down his eyes "...those trees, with that stupid ..." he was screaming with laughter now "...pair of *scissors.*" He was lying face down on the ground holding his stomach.

The Prime Minister didn't want to laugh, but deep down he had to agree with Chad. He didn't say anything though, because he knew that would upset Ebony and she was trying after all. Those scissors wouldn't have much effect on the prickly forest.

Ebony, taking absolutely no notice of Chad, proceeded to clip away at the leaves. They fell off.

Chad's mouth fell open. To his dismay the scissors were doing the job. He couldn't believe it. The leaves were falling off the trees as if it were autumn.

The Prime Minister was so overjoyed that he leapt into the air. "Yippee!" he shouted.

As Ebony snipped away at the leaves, the scissors grew in her hands until they were as large as a pair of garden shears. She was able to cut a way through the trees. The Prime Minister and Chad followed as she snipped and cut.

There was a problem however. The Prime Minister and Chad were taller than Ebony and once they started to walk into the prickly forest, they couldn't see over the tops of the trees to make sure they were going in the direction of the rock. So they turned round and came back to the tent. They tried to think of all the different ways that they could overcome this problem.

Chad said, "What we need is a ladder."

"That's very clever. Where are we going to get a ladder in the middle of nowhere?" asked Ebony.

Chad just wouldn't give up. "There must be someone nearby."

Ebony sighed. You would think that Chad, being the older one, would have a bit more sense, but it just shows you that age doesn't always mean brains!

The Prime Minister made a suggestion that Ebony thought wasn't very clever either, but out of respect to him she didn't say anything. "Perhaps we should forget about cutting a path through and crawl on our tummies. Because, as you can see, the prickly leaves don't grow down that far."

"That's a stupid idea. I think we …"

"You're so rude, Chad. The Prime Minister is trying his hardest to work things out and you're behaving in your usual ill-mannered way."

"Why is it that whatever I say is rude and stupid and whatever the Prime Minister says, even though it is stupid, you stick up for him?"

"Because the Prime Minister is THE PRIME MINISTER and you are just a stupid boy."

Chad was getting angry. "I'm fed up with you bossing me around. Give me the steel drum. I'm going home right now."

He tried to wrestle Ebony's bag from her, but the Prime Minister intervened.

"Now this is no way for cousins to behave. If it wasn't for me, I'm sure you would both injure one another. Let's not have any more fighting and arguing. Let's pool our thoughts and come up with an idea."

They thought of many different ways but, alas, none of them were really practical. Surprisingly enough, it was Chad who came up with the brainwave this time. "We should do what my friends and I do when we scrump apples from trees we can't reach."

"To be quite truthful, Chad, I think you should keep that to yourself."

Coughing, the Prime Minister said, "Ebony, I think you should give Chad a chance to add his suggestion. At the moment we are faced with an insurmountable problem and any help we can get, even though it may be small, will be good." Then he turned to Chad and said, "Proceed, boy."

Feeling very important after the Prime Minister had spoken on his behalf and put Ebony so nicely in her place, Chad made his suggestion. "I think we should sit on each other's shoulders. The person on the top should cut those leaves and the person in the middle should cut the middle leaves. Then the person on the bottom can do the bottom ones."

Throwing her head back, Ebony laughed. "That's ridiculous, whose ...?"

Holding up his finger the Prime Minister silenced Ebony. "Chad, you have proved to me today to be a boy who is a thinker. Your idea is a most excellent one. Without losing any more time, I think we should put it into practice."

"But ..." Ebony wanted to say what was wrong with the idea, but the Prime Minister walked to the edge of the forest and beckoning Chad he stooped and Chad climbed on to his shoulders. Ebony couldn't argue or complain. She had to go along with the plan. And it worked.

It took some time, but gradually the trio made a steady, straight path through the forest, without even the tiniest scratch. They slowly made their way for many miles until they suddenly came to a

clearing in the middle of the forest. In it there was a house made of sun-baked sand. It was an odd-shaped house. It had five sides and the roof was on one of the sides – instead of being on top. There were windows everywhere and on each side of the house there was a door. Out of one of these came a woman.

She stopped and looked in amazement at the trio, one on top of the other. They stopped and looked at her. She was made of fruit. Her head was the biggest grape they had ever seen and her body was like a water melon. Her arms and legs were made of bananas and her fingers and toes were made of pieces of apple. On her head she wore a straw hat.

"My word!" she exclaimed. "How did you lot get here?"

They were too astonished to answer her.

"Come in for a bite to eat and tell me all about yourselves. It's not often that I have visitors. It will make a change."

Chapter 11

The Fruit Lady was very chatty. She was just like one of those people you meet in the library or at a bus stop – you don't have to answer them because they just carry on talking. The Fruit Lady couldn't stop.

She brought out a table and some chairs and invited the three to sit down while she prepared some refreshments. All the while she chatted about the house, her family and the strange-looking animals that hung around.

Meanwhile the trio where planning what to do. "She seems a nice enough lady. She's probably lonely and is glad of some company," said Chad.

The Prime Minister and Ebony both said that they were a little uneasy about her.

"What is she doing living in the middle of nowhere? That's what I'd like to know." Ebony was suspicious of her.

"She probably doesn't want to live in the city, because it's too dirty," Chad replied.

"No, I agree with Ebony. Something isn't right. Furthermore, according to the map as I remember it, we shouldn't be too far from the gates of the palace of the city of Great Ner. She could be a spy working for King Calaloo."

Chad laughed. "Old fruitface doesn't look as though she could harm a fly. I think you and Ebony are over-reacting. Let's relax and enjoy our last moments of peace. Who knows what we have to face ahead of us?"

Chad's easy-going attitude to a difficult task made the Prime Minister all the more uncomfortable.

"I think we should be on our way," he said.

"Me too," said Ebony.

Just as she was standing up, the Fruit Lady returned. "You can't be leaving me yet, love, can you? Sit yourself down and have something to drink at least. Take the weight off your feet."

Looking at the Prime Minister, who shrugged his shoulders, Ebony sat back down again. She didn't want to have her drink, but Chad had gulped his down and the Prime Minister was sipping his. Ebony sniffed hers and then took a tiny little sip. 'It tastes good. Sort of fruity and tangy and sweet,' she thought. She was just about to sip some more when she spied the Fruit Lady standing by one of her doors peeking out at them. Then she looked at Chad and the Prime Minister. They had both fallen asleep. The Fruit Lady must have been waiting for this, because as soon as the Prime Minister began to

snore she came out of the house with two men who dragged them out of the chair and took them behind the house.

Ebony wanted to scream out, but she daren't because she wanted them to think that she too had drunk the mixture. What were they to do?

The men laid them down on the floor of a barn. The Prime Minister was at one end, Chad in the middle and Ebony at the other end. The men closed the door of the barn and Ebony heard hammers banging at the door. They were being shut in. Tears filled Ebony's eyes. To think that they had come this far, evaded all the pitfalls that King Calaloo had set for them, and then just as they were reaching their destination they had stupidly got themselves captured. Ebony tried to sit up but she couldn't do it. So she had to lie still. She thought about her mother and how she might never see her again. She thought that she would do anything to see Helen and Josette. Tied up, unable to escape and with time running out, Ebony wanted to go home. She admitted defeat. She didn't want to but what else could she do?

She wished now that she had drunk more, then she would be sleeping like Chad and the Prime Minister, without a care in the world – for a while at least.

But no. She must not give in. Ebony tried to

think what she had in her bag that could help her escape. Right now she could do with the scissors, but she didn't remember putting them back in her bag. That was a valuable lesson she had learnt. Her mother was always telling her to put things back where she got them from and now she wished that she had done just that.

She didn't even have a pair of nail clippers. If she had at least she could have snipped away at the ropes. Her nail file, which she usually carried round with her, was in the top drawer of her dresser. Fat lot of good it was doing there. "I might as well go to sleep," said Ebony aloud.

"No don't do that," squealed a voice. It was so faint Ebony could just about hear it.

"Did someone say something?" Ebony asked, her heart beating fast. She wondered if it was her imagination.

"Over here," said the voice.

She definitely heard someone that time. "Who are you? Come out and let me see you." She saw some hay in the corner move, but she couldn't see who it was.

"Here we are."

Not being able to raise her head very high made it difficult to see. Then she heard the voice, very close to her ear. "Look this way."

Turning her head, she saw a large group of ants.

It was only because they were all together that Ebony could see them at all.

"Hi! I'm Alfonso. What's your name?"

Ebony wasn't really a lover of ants, but she quickly thought that maybe – just maybe – they might help her and her friends.

"Ebony."

"Hi, Ebony," came the chorus.

"I see you're all tied up in knots," laughed Alfonso.

Ebony couldn't see what he thought was so funny but, not wanting to upset him, she laughed too. "Yeah, you could say that."

"Do you and your friends want a hand?"

Ebony replied at once, "Yes please. We need to get out of here and reach Great Ner, but we were tricked by the Fruit Lady and her friends. Now all our plans are in a mess."

"Don't you worry, we can get you out of here in no time. As for the Fruit Lady, her name is Mrs Cerpin and she belongs to the government of Great Ner. She's the right-hand man – or should I say woman – of King Calaloo. The two men are Taba and Saba."

Shockwaves washed over Ebony. They were the two men who had stolen the Mookatook bush in the first place.

"The Prime Minister was right. He didn't trust

her and neither did I. But we still drank the drink she gave us and look at the state we are in now."

Another little ant spoke up, "You've come to rescue the Mookatook bush, haven't you?"

Amazed, Ebony asked him how he knew.

"Well it figures. No one has ever got this far on their own. You must have been helped by great Lord Adonai. We have heard on the grapevine that if we meet up with you we are to give you all the help you need."

"You are so very kind."

"It's all in a day's work for us."

Alfonso said, "Now, let's work out how we are going to get you out of here and your two sleeping beauty friends."

The ants mumbled and bustled about among themselves, trying to work out a plan of action. Alfonso spoke up. "Ebony, here's what we have decided to do. All you have to do is keep still and let us do all the work."

"But tell me what you are going to do." She was frightened that they might be working for the Fruit Lady and that something worse might happen.

"Don't fret, Ebony. Trust us. We'll get you out of this."

Ebony wanted to say so much, but realised that she was unable to do a thing. 'Please,' she prayed. 'Get us out of this safely and I'll never ever be rude or bad-tempered again.' She could hear noises coming from the direction of the door. Trying to turn towards it however was a problem because of the way she was lying. What could it be? She hoped it wasn't Mrs Cerpin or Taba and Saba coming to check on their prisoners.

It wasn't them at all. It was a family of four moles. They had dug a huge hole underneath the door.

"Welcome, Ebony," said the moles.

"Hello."

It was a bit overwhelming having to speak to animals. This would never happen at home.

"Alfonso," called Ebony. "How are we going to get under the door?"

"Please trust me, Ebony, I know exactly what I am doing."

The swarm of ants gathered together in the centre of the barn. "Right lads," Ebony could hear Alfonso saying. Then the rest of his conversation was muffled. Very soon Ebony felt herself being lifted up and moved towards the door. "Alfonso, Alfonso, what's happening?" cried Ebony.

"Shush. Do you want Mrs Cerpin to find out what we are up to? Just keep quiet, will you?"

When the ants reached the door, they gently lowered Ebony underneath it. They were followed by more ants carrying Chad and the Prime Minister.

They carried them round the back of the house and back through the other side of the prickly forest. They were low enough for the prickly leaves not to harm them. The trio were carried in a single file, with Ebony in the lead and the Prime Minister at the rear.

It was a fair distance that the ants carried them, but not once did they stop and take a break. They continued until ahead of them were the most enormous gates that Ebony had ever seen in her life. The ants gently laid them down and she could hear whistling.

"Alfonso, what happens now?"

"You must learn, Ebony, not to ask too many questions. But let me tell you anyway. Ahead is your destination and I'm afraid this is where we have to leave you. Those, my dear, are the gates to the palace of Great Ner. Hah, here comes more help."

A group of small birds descended on Ebony, Chad and the Prime Minister. They were woodpeckers. They began to peck at the ropes which were tied round the trio. Once Ebony was free, she leapt up. "Oh, it's great to be free." It was fortunate that the Prime Minister and Chad had just woken up.

"Oh, my back is aching," complained the Prime Minister, rubbing his back.

"I'm not surprised," said Ebony. "We've been tied

up and carried for miles by ants. But look, we are at the entrance to the city of Great Ner."

"How did we get here?" asked Chad.

"I've just explained all that. I'm not saying it again."

Stretching and yawning, Chad said, "I could do with some more of that lovely drink the kind Fruit Lady gave us."

"She was no kind Fruit Lady. She was the wicked Mrs Cerpin who works for King Calaloo."

"No she wasn't, she …"

"Yes she was and I can prove it. Alfonso!" called Ebony. But while Ebony was talking to Chad, Alfonso, his mates and the woodpeckers had beaten a hasty retreat. "Alfonso, Alfonso."

"Who is Alfonso, Ebony? I can't see anyone here." Chad scratched his head. "Hey, how did we get here? Did the Fruit Lady arrange all this?"

By now Ebony was fed up. She quickly explained all that had happened while Chad and the Prime Minister were in a deep sleep and how they got to the gates of the city of Great Ner.

"I don't believe you," said Chad. He did half-believe Ebony because how else could they have got there without walking? But he didn't want to admit anything to her.

"I believe you," said the Prime Minister. "So far I have found you to be, among other things, an honest little girl so I'll take your word for it. Now the problem of getting here is over and with not much time left."

"Six hours to be precise," said Chad. "We had better locate the Mookatook bush and be on our way."

CHAPTER 12

The first thing that grabbed their attention was the enormous rock that almost eclipsed the palace – the rock that had guided them in the right direction. The three looked up at the gates. There were two golden lions on the top and they looked very fierce. Chad, for one, was glad that they weren't real.

There was a building, obviously the palace of King Calaloo, a good distance back from the gates. The building was so tall that you couldn't see the top because the clouds covered it.

It was very stately with a giant door made of gold. All the windows had gold round them too. On each side of the door were guards standing in a line right along the wall.

'How are we going to get past that lot?' thought Ebony. She didn't want to say anything though because the Prime Minister might become sad and Chad would want to go home.

Through the gates they could see lots and lots of people moving around. There was music playing and there were tables laden with food. Children were splashing in small swimming pools. There was excitement in the air and Ebony and Chad and even the Prime Minister wanted to join in. Everyone seemed to be very happy indeed. They were dressed in bright colours, which dazzled the trio's eyes.

Animals of all shapes and sizes – some of which Ebony and Chad knew and some they didn't – moved around freely.

"Look, there's a crocodile," pointed Chad. "Wow. He's not biting anyone!"

"There's a lion cub. Isn't he cute?" said Ebony. "He's so lovely."

The Prime Minister took out his red handkerchief and wiped his eyes. Turning to him Ebony asked, "Are you all right? Why are you crying?" she placed her hand on his arm.

He dabbed at his eyes again. "It's because they've got our Mookatook bush and this is the effect it has on a whole nation. There's peace and love and …" He sighed. " … happiness. Great Ner used to be a very war-like country. Nobody liked anybody else and they were always fighting each other. Now look at them – it's not fair."

"Well, don't you worry about that, Prime Minister, we will soon have it back." Those words of Ebony's were very brave on this side of the gate. She wasn't too sure how things would be on the other side. "What are we waiting for? Let's go in."

The gates were wide open at this time of the day. Upon entering, the Prime Minister inquired from a man who was leaning against a tree what time the gates closed. The man turned his face up to the sky and said, "About an hour's time." He smiled at the trio and then he offered them some fruit that he had in a basket by his feet.

"Er, no thank you," the Prime Minister said. "But I wonder if you could help us?"

The man came towards them smiling. "I'll try."

Clearing his throat, the Prime Minister asked him, "The Mookatook bush is, er …is …"

"On the roof of the palace. Since the King purchased it from a faraway land, our country has prospered and there is so much love between us. It's a miracle. Do you know, it used to be so hard to grow a blade of grass in Great Ner, but our King – God bless him – has enabled us to live good lives now. He is wonderful."

"Hmm, yes, yes," muttered the Prime Minister.

"What did you want to know?" asked the man.

"It's completely slipped my mind, but it was nice talking to you." They walked towards the palace.

"Now we know where it is, all we have to do is to go and get it," Ebony said.

"I think that is easier said than done," said Chad. "Look at that palace. We can't very well walk through the front door, can we?"

"No, but there must be a way in and we are going to find it."

"I have a feeling," said the Prime Minister, "that we are being watched." He was right. From one of the windows high up, a pair of binoculars were trained on them.

It was the King himself who was watching. He was so grossly overweight that his kingly robes were too tight for him, but he insisted on wearing them. His thick black hair was a mass of curls – with his crown perched on the side. On every finger was a gold ring with different coloured stones. He wore a gold chain around his neck. At one time it may have been loose but now, because he was fat, it was a little too tight. He had large, bulging eyes that grew larger when he was angry. On the mantelpiece was a large glass jar and in it were three Mookatook leaves that shone very brightly.

"So, they have managed to survive all my carefully laid plans to stop them from coming here." He turned and looked at the two men behind him, who were shaking in their boots – Taba and Saba. "So, you disposed of them, did you?"

Turning back to the window, he pointed with his finger. "Then what do I see down there? Three little busybodies, who seem to be more powerful than you." He spun round and slapped first Taba and then Saba. "How could you be so reckless? Now, if you value your lives, get rid of them because if you don't I'll get rid of you!"

They fled from the room.

The King clapped his hands and guards appeared at his side from nowhere. "I want you all to go up to the roof and protect the Mookatook bush. Now that it is mine I will never, ever let it go." He clapped his hands and the men disappeared. Training his binoculars on the trio, he said, "Now that you are in my realm, this will be the last of your days. Ha, ha, ha!" He was very confident that he could overpower them.

Standing a few metres from the entrance, the trio looked up and saw the enormity of the palace and with it the hope of ever capturing the Mookatook bush.

"We're never going to get in," said Chad.

"I fear you may be right, Chad."

Ebony spun round and faced them both. "Listen," she pointed her finger at them and spoke defiantly. "We have come too far and through too much to let this silly old building stop us from getting the Mookatook bush." Brave words.

They walked past the palace. As they reached the corner, they saw a group of men unloading from a cart large crates with straw sticking out from all sides. The men were taking them into a side door. The three didn't think twice. When the men stopped to talk to each other, Ebony, Chad and the

Prime Minister dived into a big crate. The next thing they knew they were being lifted up high.

"This one's heavy. It must have a lot of antiques in here. I don't understand what the King sees in this old bric-a-brac," said a man. "I need a bit of help with this." Another man came, took one side of the crate and carried it into the palace.

Just then a handful of guards rushed past the men and ran to the front of the building. Leading them were Taba and Saba.

"Where they did go?" asked Taba.

"They must be here somewhere," Saba replied hopefully.

"We'd better find them, otherwise we'll be in big trouble."

Faintly, the trio could hear them talking to the guards, so they kept very quiet. Unfortunately, some of the straw tickled Chad's nose. He sneezed.

"Did you hear something?" one of the men said.

"Yeah I did. It sounded like someone sneezing."

The trio held their breaths. It would be dreadful if they were discovered now.

Suddenly they felt the crate going down and then it bumped on to the floor. They heard voices talking. "Sh!" said the Prime Minister.

"Don't leave the crates here, put them on the pulley."

More gruff voices. They felt the crate being lifted

again and then dumped down. They heard creaking and felt the crate being raised upwards.

"I think we're in a lift," said Chad. "I wonder where we will end up?"

He didn't have to wonder for very long. The creaking stopped and someone said, "Your Royal Highness, where would you like the crate placed?"

The King took a while to answer. It seemed like forever to the trio. Then he said, "Put it in the middle of the room and take my precious possessions out."

He didn't say please or thank you!

From their hiding place beneath the straw they heard the King's command. The Prime Minister began to perspire through fear. Chad demanded the steel drum from Ebony – now was the time to go home. But Ebony said, "As soon as they lift the straw up, we have to make a run for it. Now don't argue, just do it."

There was no time to lose. As the layers of straw were taken out of the crate, Ebony counted to three. Then, followed by Chad and the Prime Minister, she burst out of the crate, taking the occupants of the room by surprise. They headed for the door, but just before Chad grabbed the doorknob, it opened. There were Taba and Saba and the guards, reluctantly ready to report to the King their failure to find the trio – and here they were!

Taba and Saba wasted no time in taking control

of the situation. They took hold of Chad by the scruff of his neck and some of the guards held Ebony by her waist as she kicked and struggled to be free. The Prime Minister was held by his arms. They were all prisoners.

CHAPTER 13

The King sat on his throne. He was very satisfied with the events of the day. Ebony, Chad and the Prime Minister were standing in front of him, awaiting punishment.

" ...So you see it was pure folly to come to my kingdom and try to steal my Mookatook bush. Very stupid. Did you not know of my fame? I am the Great King Calaloo of Great Ner whose power is mightier than any other. Did not the King and Queen of Merari tell you what you would be up against? Ha! Well now, all that is in the past. I'm happy to say that you have failed in your attempt to win back what is rightfully mine and ..."

The Prime Minister couldn't stand hearing the proud boasts of the King. He shouted, "The Mookatook bush does not belong to you. You are a thief and a liar and I hope you rot in ..."

"Silence, little man, or else I will have your tongue removed."

Ebony was about to say something, but when she heard the King's threat to the Prime Minster she thought it best to keep quiet.

The King's eyes were bulging out of his head and a deep frown creased his forehead, knitting his eyebrows together. He did look fearsome.

"Remove these tiresome creatures from my sight until I can think up a terrible way to remove them forever."

The guards led them out of the room and up some stairs. By the time they had climbed enough stairs to be halfway to the moon, the Prime Minister was finding it difficult to catch his breath.

"I say, do you think …" He took a deep breath. " …we could stop for a moment?"

Taba said to two of the guards, "Carry him the rest of the way." The two guards hoisted the Prime Minister up on to their shoulders for the remainder of the journey.

After walking down a long corridor, they finally came to a small room.

"In you go, and this time there will be no escaping," laughed Saba.

Stumbling one after the other, the trio were pushed into the dark room. There was no window but there was a hatch-door in the ceiling – far too high to reach. They could hear the key being turned in the door.

"That's it then," said Chad cheerfully.

"What are you so happy about? There's no way we are going to get out of this room."

"Oh yes there is," said Chad.

"How?"

"I've been saying it all along. We need to play the steel drum."

"How can we? It's too late now. We'd be able to get out, but what about the Prime Minister?"

"He can come with us."

Pacing the room, Ebony was getting angry. "I don't think the Prime Minister would somehow fit into my family, do you?" Then, turning to the Prime Minister, "I don't mean to be rude, but it's the truth."

"I fully understand your reasoning, Ebony. Although I would like to add that there is another consideration. Lord Adonai has been fully aware of our circumstances throughout this mission. I'm sure he knows of our unfortunate imprisonment. We may get out of here yet."

"Well, let's hope he does something within the next two and a half hours, otherwise Ebony and I are in a right pickle."

Silence pervaded the room. Ebony continued to pace up and down. The Prime Minister and Chad sat on the floor. The minutes ticked by. The room became hot and the Prime Minister's feather which had already taken such a beating was wilting.

That first hour was the longest hour of their lives. Ebony's mind was ticking like a bomb ready to explode and the Prime Minister was secretly hoping and praying that Lord Adonai would come to the rescue. Chad was dreaming of the swimming baths and his first dive into the water.

"I've just thought of something."

"Yes?" piped up the Prime Minister. He was ready to try anything.

"Remember how we cut our way through the prickly forest? We can do the same thing again. If we sit on each other's shoulders we might be able to reach the hatch-door."

The Prime Minister stood up quickly. He thought it was a great idea. So did Chad, but he didn't want to show it.

"Okay," he drawled. "We can try. If it doesn't work, it doesn't work." He threw his arms up into the air.

The Prime Minister bent down while Chad got on to his shoulders. Then it was Ebony's turn. She stretched her hands up but she couldn't quite reach the door.

"Oh no, I can't open it," she cried.

"Don't panic," said the Prime Minister. He was trying his hardest to keep still but he was finding it difficult and was tottering around a little.

Chad said, "Why don't you take off your shoe and see if that reaches the door?"

"Good idea," said Ebony.

It was a bit tricky to raise her leg and slip her

Kicker boot off, but she managed to do it. And sure enough she reached the door with it. With some force, she levered the door open. Welcoming her was the sky.

"This room leads to the roof," cried Ebony in surprise.

"What a perfect situation," agreed the Prime Minister. "Quickly, get out, Ebony. Let's get the Mookatook bush."

Ebony stood on Chad's shoulders and clambered through the hatch-door and on to the roof. She took a few deep breaths. It was wonderful to be inhaling fresh air once again. There was a garden on the roof with trees and plants of all kinds.

Next, it was Chad's turn. He stood on the Prime Minister's shoulders and with help from Ebony scrambled up.

Soon they were both out in the open air. Getting the Prime Minister out would not be so easy. He was too short to reach the hatch-door.

"Children, I think you will have to take the Mookatook bush yourselves and return it to the King and Queen." He was very sad.

"No, we can't go without you," replied Ebony. "We will find a way."

"Can't you try and jump up high and see if we can catch you?" asked Chad.

"Honestly, Chad, I don't know where you get

such ideas. That won't work," said Ebony.

"Is there anything in the garden that could help get me out of here?" said the Prime Minister.

At once, Ebony and Chad darted round the garden looking for something that would get the Prime Minister out.

They found a long rubber hose attached to the floor of the roof. The hose unwound as they carried it back to the hatch-door.

"C'mon, Prime Minister. Climb up."

His first few attempts were unsuccessful. He kept slipping back down again. Chad said to the Prime Minister, "Take your shoes and socks off and then you'll be able to grip the hose with your bare feet."

The Prime Minister was halfway up the hose when the door opened and the guards rushed in.

"Quick," shouted Ebony. "Hurry."

Struggling very hard, the Prime Minister tried to climb faster. The first guard began to climb the hose, trying to get hold of the Prime Minister's ankle. The other guards began shouting and arguing and some of them left the room.

"Hurry, hurry," cried Ebony.

"Quick, give me your arm," said Chad.

The Prime Minister's heart was beating fast. He was climbing the hose with all his might – his life depended on it!

As he neared the door, both Ebony and Chad,

lying flat on the ground, leaned down and grabbed the Prime Minister. Together they dragged him up to safety.

When the Prime Minister found his feet, he didn't have time to put his socks and shoes on. He left them in his pocket. "We have to find the Mookatook bush."

It didn't take them long. The leaf that Ebony had in her bag began to hum and the bright rays from the leaves, even in the day, helped the trio to locate its whereabouts. The Prime Minister started digging with a spade that he had found.

Ebony and Chad stood in front of the bush. For a moment they admired its beauty. "It's gorgeous," whispered Ebony.

Behind them they heard a noise. The guards had alerted the King and he and his men were advancing rapidly.

Wasting no more time, the Prime Minister uprooted the Mookatook bush and ran. Ebony and Chad were right behind. The guards were shouting to each other to corner the trio. They soon discovered that there was no place to run to. They were trapped like animals. The King stepped forward. "You didn't think that you were going to get away, did you?" Then his tone changed and he became very menacing. "Give me my bush."

The Prime Minister held on to the Mookatook

bush. He was determined not to give it up without a fight.

"You're not going to have it," shouted Ebony.

Chad joined in. "It's not yours."

The King and the guards moved closer to the trio, who squeezed their backs against the wall. The guards were closing in. Ebony was the first to step on to the wall, followed by the Prime Minister holding on to the Mookatook bush, and then Chad.

The clouds were like large bunches of cottonwool that were tangled up in Ebony's hair. She looked down. The ground was miles and miles away.

"Don't come any closer," said the Prime Minister.

"Why not?" said the King.

"Because we will jump."

No one said a word. The silence was ominous. The King stepped closer, with his guards standing near.

The Prime Minister looked at Ebony and then at Chad. There was only one course of action. "One, two, three …jump!" shouted the Prime Minister.

As they plunged over the edge, they glanced back to see the King and his guards looking down at them. "Get them!" ordered the King.

The light breeze caught hold of Ebony's dress and as she glided down, the dress opened up like a parachute. Chad was holding on to one of her arms, the Prime Minister the other. The people on the

ground looked up in amazement as they sailed down.

Some of the guards at the entrance to the palace rushed forward ready to recapture Ebony, her cousin and her friend.

Halfway down, they began to speed up. More guards came out of the palace. The Mookatook bush was weighing the Prime Minister down. He was pulling away from Ebony. He was some way from the outstretched arms of the guards when the trio suddenly found themselves being lifted back up again. They heard the people *ohhh*ing and *ahhh*ing. Things were happening quickly.

They were sitting on something that was warm and soft, yet managing to stay in the air. It was a giant eagle that had come to their rescue.

"Thank you, Lord Adonai," screamed Ebony in delight. By now they all knew that Lord Adonai had once again come to give them aid.

The large bird soared through the sky, climbing higher and higher. Within a short while, the eagle flew over the rocks where they had hidden their boat. The bird didn't stop. As they looked down, they could see that some people had gathered near the boat ready to stop them from leaving. The bird, with wings outstretched, flew confidently and effortlessly across the sea. The Prime Minister could not stop smiling. He held on to the Mookatook bush lovingly. It was so peaceful up in the air that the children soon dropped off to sleep.

They awoke with a bump. "Wake up, my dears. We have returned safely to Merari."

CHAPTER 14

The King and Queen and all their royal subjects were standing on the beach, awaiting their arrival. As soon as the Prime Minister stepped down from the eagle with the Mookatook bush in his hand, the darkness began to fade away. He ran with the bush to its original "home" and, with care and attention, replanted it.

The dark oppressiveness of Merari vanished in a flash. Beaming smiles returned to the people. Their skin was no longer shrivelled and dry, but glowing and soft and smooth.

"Hurrah!" they shouted.

"Three cheers for the Prime Minister!"

"Hip, hip, hurray."

Ebony and Chad stood back, watching the people of Merari enjoy their happiness. Children were running around and even the animals got caught up in the joy. Some of the adults began to play instruments and when they brought out some steel drums, Ebony couldn't resist. She began to sing:

"Love and happiness everywhere
Say goodbye to all your fears
The Mookatook bush belongs right here
Let's sing and dance – we have no cares!"

The King and Queen, with their crowns wobbling on their heads ,joined in with the dancing. The Prime Minister's feather straightened up and he too flung his arms and legs about in time to the music.

Chad was looking at his watch and trying to get hold of Ebony's attention. She was busily involved with the people who were dancing to the music and the words of her song. Chad pulled Ebony's arm and whispered to her, "We only have five minutes left."

She didn't take any notice of him. And what made it worse, the people had brought out a limbo stick and were in the process of setting it up. This increased Ebony's excitement. She wasn't interested in what Chad wanted to say. This was the life for her.

Ebony didn't even notice that Chad, with some difficulty, was removing the steel drum from her bag. A young girl asked Ebony if she would like to go under the stick first. Singing her song, Ebony began to move towards the stick.

Meanwhile, Chad held the steel drum and was quickly walking towards Ebony. As she came out from under the stick, Chad began to play the drum. The atmosphere was charged with electricity. Ebony held on to Chad and continued to dance and sing:

"Love and happiness everywhere
Say goodbye to all your fears …"

She wasn't able to get any further, because she and Chad began to spin wildly. It was difficult for them to catch their breath. Suddenly, there was a noise like a rocket launching and Ebony and Chad were lifted up out of sight. There was no time to say goodbye.

Sitting on the floor in a heap, Ebony and Chad looked at each other. Ebony was just about to say something when her mother called out to her. "Ebony! Stop all that fooling around down there. Come upstairs and do something useful for a change. Give me a hand with the beds."

Ebony wanted to burst out laughing. If only her mother knew where she and Chad had been! She wouldn't believe them!

Ebony hoped that she would meet up with her new-found friends again, if only to say goodbye. You never know, it could happen!